The Driver

Meg Barber

Also by Meg Barber

The Causton Series: (Regency Romance)

The Army's Daughter

The Army's Son

Chantel

Elena

Samantha

Montana Love (A Modern Romance)

Dear Reader

'Leave a review, feed an author', has more than a grain of truth in it. If there is anything you enjoyed about the book, please say so, either on Goodreads (free and open to anyone) or on Amazon if you bought the book there or read it on Kindle Unlimited. Writing is an unpaid labour of love, and the reward is other people enjoying the story. If you wish to be informed when the next book is available, please send your email to authormegbarber@yahoo.com. You will not be bombarded with emails; I have neither the technical know-how to do that, nor the time. That is a promise. When people say that they like my stories, I light up like a neon sign, so if you praise The Driver, glance out of the window; there is a multi-coloured glow out there somewhere.

Happy reading.

Part One

Chapter One

I fall forward and let gravity take me. I descend stairs the same way I do mountains, without thought, tipping into space and letting my feet tap lightly on each step on the way down. At the bottom there is a small square lobby, little wider than my shoulders, with a door on the right to the outside and a door to my left to the luxury garage area. Above me is my domain. A large rectangular space with a bed, a large window with a blind, a kitchen with a hob, microwave and kettle, bathroom, and a seating and eating area. Plain and functional. I find the sparse white and grey space soothing. Anyone else might describe it as bleak. But I have known poverty and hardship. And now I know luxury. And luxury is heating, cleanliness and privacy.

When I step into the garage area I don't bother hitting the lights. Seven luxury cars stretch out before me, gleaming in the dull early light. Moving into the centre of the space, I blip a black behemoth and slip into the driving seat. As the garage door lifts, I slide the car forward and stop a little to the right of the front steps of the house. The boss likes to look down and gaze at his possessions, the car and me, as he readies himself for the day. I don't question orders. Not simple ones like these. I just do as I am told. And every morning I do this is another night I have survived.

I have already eaten so I stand silent and upright for twenty minutes or so until the boss appears, the gun in my shoulder holster hidden behind my suit jacket the knife strapped to my calf. I wear the gun. But it gets pointed where he demands.

Chapter Two

My working hours are uneven and I am lonely. It isn't exactly as if I can join a, I don't know, hobby group, or frequent a local pub. At first I remained solitary filling the time with working out and reading, but lately I have taken to sitting in cafes. The ones in Kensington are always buzzing with people and it helps to take the edge off my isolation. It is one of those bright English days where the sun is around but choosy about when to appear, and the air has a chill to it. I stand in the doorway blocking the light and check who is in there. It all looks safe enough. A man stands collecting his backpack and phone and heads towards me so, as there is at least one spare seat, I go and order a coffee. I carry it across to the vacated seat, and slide into position. There are four chairs around the table; a student type hunched over his keyboard, hair obscuring his face is diagonally opposite, a girl has reversed her chair so that she is looking out at the room is on my immediate left, and a woman, leaning deep over her coffee is directly in front of me. As I sit the girl on my left smiles up at me, but I ignore her. She is too young and too fashionable. Perhaps at first glance I may look like the sort of man she is hunting for, but she has no idea how wrong she is. She pouts with irritation at my lack of response, which makes me bury my face into my coffee. I want to smile with amusement at her behaviour but don't want to encourage her.

I put my coffee down on the table and shove my chair back with a screech of its legs. I am beginning to wonder if I should copy the girl and sit facing outwards when the woman opposite looks up. She quickly dips her face again. She is crying, hiding behind a fall of thick, glossy hair the colour of the hazelnuts I fought the squirrels for as a child. I still have a foolish addiction to hazelnuts. Beside me the girl stands with a huff and grabs her handbag. She stalks out and I give her back view a quick glance. It is a good one, but she is wobbling on stilt-high stilettos. I am not immune to long, lean, legs in high heels, but the woman in them needs to know how to walk without looking as if she might topple over at any minute. I give in to my amusement and take a sip of coffee. This is why I come out to cafes, I can people watch and feel a part of the life around me. Even if I am not. Then the boy opposite sweeps back his hair with a dramatic gesture, grabs at his belongings and dashes out, nearly knocking a chair over. Now I have to grin. Was the girl's smile to me intended to make him jealous? Pay attention?

I breathe in, feeling content for the moment. Now there is just the crying woman and me at the table, and when another couple of people leave the noise level drops noticeably. I drink my coffee slowly, mostly watching a group of young women with little ones in buggies. They are laughing and look happy to be in each other's company. I am not looking at the sad woman. Staying sitting here gives her some privacy; I am not known for my daintiness. I hear her take in a breath, and then she stands. She pushes her hair away from her face, picks up her phone, and moves away from the table. Close up, there is a woman I could be attracted to. Her hair, now I can see it better, falls in heavy waves past her shoulders and her lips are full and soft and do not look injected with plastic. She passes by me without looking at me. I give her a moment and then rise and follow her.

She is standing in the street just outside the café as if she does not know where to go. I touch her lightly on the shoulder.

'Lady,' I say, 'I know I am a big strange man, but will you walk with me a little?' Huge brown eyes stare up at me full of uncertainty. Her mouth opens a little, but she says nothing. 'Sometimes we all need a shoulder to cry on or perhaps a bit of company. The street is full of people, and I mean you no harm.' I keep my voice gentle, and hope my eyes show her that I really am of no danger to her.

She shrugs and turns away, and as she hasn't told me to mind my own business, I stay beside her. I am useful, I think, as my bulk carves a path through the bustle of the High Street. We cross the road and soon I can see Holland Park ahead. She walks towards the grass and sits on a bench at the edge of the park. Dozens of people are bustling around us with their eyes on their phones or into the middle distance as if gazing ahead will get them somewhere faster.

'Who are you?' she asks abruptly.

'My name is Marco Ilîc, I am Serbian, so from a beautiful country, and I watched as a lovely lady tried to swallow her tears and I wanted to offer comfort, if only for a minute.'

'Why would you do that?'

I give her a wry smile and shrug, 'Perhaps because there have been times in my life when a little comfort would have been welcome. Will you tell me what is wrong?'

She looks down at her linked hands causing her hair to fall forward and hide her face again, but I see the tear that falls onto them. Then she throws her head back and her face is working in an attempt to control the pain she is feeling. Her mouth is open as if she would scream, and her throat is so tight it could probably rival steel. Saying nothing, I lay my big hand over her two small ones giving her my warmth. I am half turned towards her and to my surprise she rocks forward, rests her head onto my left shoulder just under my collar bone, and begins to sob. Slowly and gently I rub her back with my other hand but otherwise just let her lean onto me; she is not restrained in anyway. We sit there as all the busy people ignore us and she cries out whatever it is that pains her. Eventually, she pulls away.

'I am so sorry,' she says, swallowing. She is searching for a handkerchief so I hand her my packet of tissues that were squashed into my back pocket. She smiles, and begins to scrub her face. Clearly, she is too embarrassed to look at me.

'Hey,' I say softly, and she finally turns to meet my eyes. 'It is okay. You don't know me, you will never see me again, but for the moment, I am here for you.' I smile gently, wondering if she can see the loneliness that lives inside of me. Her touch was the first innocent human contact I have felt in a long, long while.

'Oh!' she says, covering her mouth with her hand. 'I have soaked your tee shirt. You really did give me a shoulder to cry on.'

'Do you feel a bit better?' When she nods I say, 'Then a little bit of wet will do no harm.'

'It is such a silly thing.'

'What is?' I wonder, but it is up to her what she tells me.

'You will think me a fool.'

'I think that you are a very beautiful woman who this afternoon is for some reason very sad. Will you tell me why?'

She stares across the park and I think that perhaps, now she has let out her sadness, I should go. I begin to shift my weight when without looking at me she says, 'I live alone and I have few friends, but I did have a cat. She was called Misty, and I loved her. I would catch the Tube home and then walk towards my street. There was a low brick wall on the corner and every single day of her life she would be sitting there, paws so neatly together, waiting for me. Every day. Without fail. At night she would curl up next to me while I worked or watched television, and at night she would nose under my duvet and burrow against me and go to sleep. I have just come from the vets where I had not only to put her to sleep, but leave her body as I have no garden to bury her in.' The tears begin to slide again. 'And I can't help it, I just miss her so much.'

This time I reach for her and pull her gently into my body. I wrap my arms around her and hold her close, leaning my chin over her head so that she will feel enclosed and safe. When, finally, she pulls away she lifts a wrecked face to me and says, 'You smell very nice.'

It is so not what I expected, I burst out with a laugh. 'Good,' I say.

Again she wipes her face dry. It will be some time before all those tears are spent, I think. 'Come, let's take you for a walk.'

'Like a dog on a lead?' she teases.

I grin at her. 'Something like that.' I stand, and offer her my hand. She lets me lift her to her feet and then she steps away.

'Marco,' she says with a frown.

'That's right,' I nod.

She holds out her hand, 'Evie Scott. I am very pleased to meet you.'

I am grinning as I shake her hand in a formal fashion. She seems to have begun to trust me, at least here, in the open, with many people around.

'How long are you in London for?' she asks.

'I live here now.' And will die here too, I think.

'What do you do?'

I grin at her. 'I may be Serbian, but I am legal. I have all the correct documents.'

She goes bright red. 'Oh, I am so sorry, I didn't mean that! I just wondered if you were working here on, oh, I don't know, a specific project or something?'

'Like a building site?' I am teasing her, and at last she begins to realise it. She shakes her head but she is grinning back at me. 'I was a lorry driver,' I begin, 'I travelled all over Europe. I saw many places and met many people, but now I drive a rich man around in his big shiny cars.'

'Shiny cars,' she echoes, and her grin turns wry. 'Did you prefer the lorries?'

'They needed a lot less polishing and, believe me, I was proud of my lorries, I liked them to look smart. Very smart.'

She gives another huge grin, 'Was there lots of chrome and bright red paintwork?'

'Of course,' and I keep my voice serious, but my eyes are dancing. I have made her smile, and I am glad.

Finally, I can see that she has relaxed. We walk around some of the paths in the park and she allows me to buy her an ice cream. I watch her put out her tongue like a little cat to tease a morsel away from the cone and into her mouth. I am thinking of exactly where else I would like that small, pink tongue, but have the grace to look away out over the trees that surround us. If she could read my mind she would run away and completely forget the ice cream.

She tells me about what she likes about London, and what she doesn't. She quizzes me on what sights I have seen and tells me off when she learns that I have not been to the Tower of London. I don't like to tell her that I am afraid that if I went Hohne might want me to bring the crown jewels back with me. And I am only half joking. I do gain some credit for having been to Tower Bridge and being able to tell her all about the lifting mechanism and how ships request permission to pass through.

'I am very good with a spanner,' I tell her with a serious face. She looks at me for a moment frowning, then tips back her head and laughs. It is the best afternoon I have ever had in London. Eventually, we begin to amble back to Kensington High Street. Our afternoon is over.

We walk along the streets until she finds the right bus stop. She is looking better, little Evie. That deep sadness has lifted for a while from her shoulders and I feel a buzz of pleasure that I may have helped that to happen. The walk outside, with people rushing around has also helped, I think. And then I realise what I wish to ask and I am astonished at myself. So much so, a bubble of laughter rises in my chest. I have stopped, like a rock in a river, forcing pedestrians to change pace and direction to avoid me. Evie has stopped also, and I shelter her from the shoving with my body. Looking up at me, she frowns and asks,

'What?'

How can I tell her that I feel in that moment like a scabbed kneed schoolboy, back in the dusty streets of my childhood, waiting for my mother to call me for supper. A small laugh escapes me.

'What?' Evie asks again, and her mouth is curling in echo of mine.

'I want,' I begin, 'I want to ask if you go to the café often?' And now my smile is huge as I say it.

'You are asking me if I come here often?'

I can feel laughter bubbling, 'Uh huh,' I agree. And now she is smiling widely.

'And that makes you laugh?'

Hell yes, but how can I explain? I haven't been with a woman for over three years, and before that my question would usually be, my place or yours?

She looks away out over the street to the upper level of the buildings that line the high street on the other side. They are a typical muddle of brick and stone facings, unpainted wood and glossy facades. The view ebbs and flows into sight as a red bus edges its way through traffic and cars angle and finesse their way towards their destinations. I breathe in the hot, stale air, full of the taste of traffic, and know that I will remember this foolish moment forever.

'Sometimes,' she says, not looking at me.

'Ah.' I take it as a dismissal. 'It's ok, I understand. Can I walk you anywhere? I need to head back to work.'

'You have a job?'

'Yes, but the hours are irregular. I have most afternoons off.' Already I am pushing it. I can't afford to be late for Hohne.

'Wednesdays, sometimes,' she says, and looks up at me, frowning. She glances up the street. We are a few paces from a bus stop. 'That is my bus.' She points to a double decker crawling towards us.

'Farewell, little Evie,' I say. 'I hope I see you again.'

She darts me a small smile and a nod, a dismissal, and takes a few steps towards where the bus will stop, edging into the huddle of other people already waiting. I stand, getting in people's way, until I see her climb on board. She gives a quick turn and her eyes meet mine for the briefest of moments before she is pushed further into the bus entrance. She looked back. I hold that thought, not sure if it means something or not. Then, finally, I join the flow of people and hasten my steps so I will not be late reporting for duty.

. . .

Two nights have passed since I met Little Evie. And both times I fell asleep with her face in my mind, especially that last glance back. Might she go to the café next Wednesday in the hope of meeting me? One thing I am certain of, it is where I am spending my next Wednesday afternoon, that is, if Hohne doesn't need me. It is late and I am roaming the apartment, rinsing a mug, placing a new tube of toothpaste handy, thinking about sleep, when the hairs on the back of my neck go up. I pull off my jumper so I am dressed only in a black tee shirt and dark trousers. My knife is still strapped to my calf and I slide the gun into the back waistband of my trousers and ammo into a pocket. I don't touch the lights; let anyone out there think I am still in here. Nothing I can do if my shadow could be seen and now has disappeared. I put on the bathroom light in the hopes they think I might have moved to there and slide out of the fire escape door that leads off the kitchen area. I go out as low as possible and creep down the stairs silently. At the bottom I slide behind the shrubbery and head for the outer wall. Hohne has at least three men inside, possibly nine, and me outside. My job is to make the exterior safe; the others keep Hohne safe. The spider in his web. And now, one of the strands has been tugged.

At the back wall I begin a slow circuit, checking outwards all the while towards the house to see if I can spot any intruders. I may just be being a complete idiot. I have no idea what alarmed me, all I know is that I feel unsettled. The grounds are full of large shrubs, but spaced apart, each standing sentinel on its own. Some are cut into fancy shapes; not my style, I prefer natural or plain trims. I am just thinking that, yes, I am an idiot and staring at a huge green bush, when I realise that the smooth shape has just grown a round shape on its arse. Now, that wasn't there before. At that moment the moon goes behind a cloud and the outline becomes too dark to see. I edge forward, placing each foot down as precisely as possible. I leave the gun in my waistband, one bullet and the police will be here in minutes; this is a neighbourhood the police are acutely aware of. My knife is now in my right hand, my arm forward of my body. I'd rather the tip of my knife found an obstacle than a clumsy arm or foot of mine. All around me are dark and deeper dark and lighter shadows, a play of confusion on the senses. Any one of these obscure patches between the treasured shrubs could be another man, or the first one who has changed positions.

And then the moon reappears and I am within a metre of the man, and he is intent on the house and not on me creeping up from behind. I reach and shove the tip of my knife into the side of his neck, where the carotid artery pumps away.

'Silence,' I hiss. 'Bend down and take off your shoe.'

I sense his uncertainty. I suspect he thinks I want his shoes off so running away will be harder, but he does I say. Already I know he is an amateur. A pro would have spun away from the knife and down with a good chance of breaking my hold, especially here in the night where the man in front of me is no more than dark air.

When the shoe is off and with me crouching behind him, I tell him to pull off his sock and stuff it in his mouth. He begins to protest but I push the knife in and the blood trickling down his neck increases enough for him to do as I say. With my left hand I now shove the barrel of the gun into the notch at the base of his scull while with my right I find plastic ties for his wrists. That done, I use two to keep his ankles in place then another to link his hands and fasten them to a low branch. It is three centimetres, if that, in width, but it is amazing the strength vegetation can have. I roll him partially under the huge bush. Picking up my knife I take out the sock and hiss, 'How many are you?'

'Nine,' he spits, so I shove the sock back in and stand. I look down at him for a moment. I think nine is unlikely. He seems to be the only outer guard. As I believe he had lied to me, I boot his head hard and roll him further under the shrub and shove some leaves over him. He won't come to for a while.

I return to the outer wall and circumnavigate the house. I see no other intruders and begin to edge inwards towards the house when blue lights appear outside the metal gates. Taking a chance there really is no one else in the grounds I jog towards them and hit the entry button and five black vehicles slide silently in. I slide my gun and knife into deep leaves under a laurel and feel sick. The British police are some of the best trained that there are. When stopping a young moron for driving without insurance or driving while under the influence of drink or drugs, they approach like a friendly neighbour, all, 'Hi mate, what's your name? This your vehicle is it?' They seem like cuddly harmless teddy bears, and they don't usually need to be any tougher. Everyone knows that they are unarmed and rarely use their tasers or batons, so it all stays pretty low key. But play them up, and you will find yourself with six on top of you and being shoved into a van with handcuffs on. However, one breath of a gun or knife and the guys with huge guns, riot gear and faces covered in masks will take you and your house or vehicle apart at the seams. Their dogs are superbly trained to sniff out weapons, drugs, money and goodness knows what else.

By contrast I saw a video on YouTube where a black guy in the US was watering the front flower beds for an old white couple who were away. A white neighbour called the police, like you do when a man has a hose and is watering pretty flowers. I mean, exactly how threatening is that behaviour? When the police cruiser arrived they came in hard, 'What's your name, do you live here?' and so on. The guy was standing there holding a hose! Their attitude immediately put up the back of gardening guy as he knew that they were only there as he was black. He ended up in handcuffs! For being a nice guy and decent neighbour. I put that down to lack of training. Those guys could learn something from the Brits.

So, I have my hands in the air just in case, but I am relaxed. This is not the States. No one is going to shoot me. A guy is shouting at me that he is the police and I am to stand still, so I do. Bit obvious, I think, I mean, who else appears with blue disco lights, big dark vans full of guys with in black with big guns and Police written all over them. But like I know, they are trained and they follow procedures. Usually.

One steps across to speak to me, 'Evening sir, and who are you?'

'I am Mr Hohne's driver. I saw the lights and ran down to let you in. What is going on?'

'You don't know?'

'I live above the garage, there.' I point to the building behind us, a

14

seven-car garage with the lights from my apartment at the end still shining.

'Ok, sir, go and sit with this officer here while we see what is going on inside the house.'

Already half of the force have vanished searching the grounds with flashlights. I can see the bright lights bobbing and weaving. Shit, I think, just how far under that bush did I shove the guy I found? Was it far enough? If not, I am going to have some wriggling to do. He has a cut on his neck just under the artery that is probably still bleeding. Hardly a shaving nick. Did I kick him hard enough to kill him, or just knock him out? Head wounds are always uncertain.

It takes a couple of hours and I am stuck sitting in the back of a locked police car with nothing to do except look out of a misty wind-screen. And then it is all over. Vans and cars begin to reverse out of the drive and I am released.

'You are free to go, Mr Ilîc. Your employer has vouched for you.' Behind me, three men are being 'escorted' in handcuffs, into a large van.

That is good, I think. You never know with Hohne. I jog up towards the house where the huge steel-reinforced front door is fully open and every room is alight.

I stride in. Hohne is right in front of me, three of his acolytes around him. All three are senior to me; they have all been with Hohne for years and live in the main house on an upper floor. I also suspect that they know what Hohne's business really is and do his dirty work. I am kept out over the garage and am told nothing, which I am very happy about.

'What happened?' I ask.

DePaul, the most senior of the guys answers, 'What is it to you and where the fuck were you?'

I stare him down. 'I was checking the grounds. All of it, on my own it seems. What were you three doing? How did those men get in the house?' I am trying not to sound angry, but failing to keep it out of my voice.

It is Hohne who takes the sting out of the confrontation. 'They got in through a pantry window. I didn't even know that we had a pantry.'

'How far did they get?' I ask.

Hohne shrugs, 'Not far. Donner and Manon caught them before they got through the kitchen.'

'All three?' Donner nods as if he is a Labrador who has returned his ball. 'So why the hell were the police called? We could have dealt with this internally.' I can't hide the anger from my voice.

I feel Hohne's eyes on me as DePaul steps towards me. 'He is right,' Hohne says. 'It was a mistake.'

I look at Hohne, 'Do you know who sent them? They were amateurs, not pros.'

'How do you know that?' demands DePaul.

'Because the one I took down was no professional.'

'What one?' It is Manon shoving his oar in now, the third goon.

'The one I have trussed up under a bush outside,' I tell him. 'If you don't know who sent them, perhaps we ought to question the only one we have left.' My voice drips with sarcasm. I expect a slap-down from Hohne, but he just nods. 'Bring him into the kitchen. The floor is easily cleaned there.' He turns and walks away. 'You three,' he calls back over his shoulder without slowing, 'Get back to your duties.' The three all sneer, but gradually edge away, walking backwards, until they too seem to realise how ridiculous they look and vanish in various directions. I draw in a breath. I am not being party to a murder, however much Hohne pays me. That guy outside is a patsy. An idiot who was paid to cause a ruckus, at a guess, rattle Hohne's cage but do no real harm. I turn, and head out into the cold of the night to unearth my gun and knife before I release the fool from his nest of leaves.

To some relief I find that he is awake. I heard him as I got close as he was rubbing his head around attempting to get rid of the sock. As I pull it out he mutters, 'That was a real dirty trick, that was.' I grin and slice through the ankle ties before I haul him up and fireman fashion throw him over my shoulder. He doesn't weigh that much, which reinforces my view that this guy is only a young idiot who thinks he is on

the conveyor belt to criminal mastermind. The world is full of delu-
sional undereducated boys like this. They rarely make anything worth-
while of their lives and I pity them, almost as much as I pity myself. I
didn't even have dreams of being a criminal, yet here I am.

In the kitchen I dump the lad on a chair and lean back against the
near wall, crossing my arms so that my biceps flex. If the way I carried
him so easily and the size of my arms don't impress on him how
outclassed he is, he is even more stupid than I think he is. Hohne flicks
me a glance.

'You can leave now,' he tells me.

'Find out where he is from and I will drop him off close enough so
that he can walk home. Damage him too much, and I will go straight to
the police. I am not going to jail because those three idiots put us on the
police radar.'

Hohne stares at me with fury, and then his face relaxes. 'You can
have him in an hour. Take the Mercedes.'

I nod, and head back to my apartment. Once inside I pace. It is bad
enough being employed by Hohne, but up to now he has been careful
to keep me away from what he really does and I could go along with
that. My head is spinning. Why were the police called? When they
arrived they had all lights flashing, but there were no sirens. Why was
that? Does the Chief of the Met live down the road? I doubt it, as most
of this part of London is multi-millionaires only. I take some deep
breaths and then stretch each part of my body in turn. Weights are all
very well, but without flexibility exercises like yoga or Pilates, it is too
easy to become muscle-bound and lose mobility. I try to concentrate on
the exercises, but my mind is worrying at what is going on in the main
house like a dog with a bone. When the hour is up, I cross the drive
back and head around to the kitchen door. The main door is now firmly
shut and most of the house lights are off. Hohne is in the kitchen and
apart from a black eye, which in all honesty I may have given him, the
lad looks fine.

'Drop him off in central Luton,' Hohne instructs. Luton is some
miles north of London and an easy run north up the motorway. I nod

and taking the boy by the arm, head him back out into the night. When we get to the Merc he says excitedly, 'Can I sit in the back.' I look down at him. 'No. You sit in the front where I can see you. Do I need to hand-cuff you?'

'Nah, honest. I'm just grateful for the lift, you know? My mum will be worried sick.'

Hell, I think. When I kicked him in the head to keep him quiet I never thought of an anxious mum back home somewhere staring at a clock. 'Get in,' I say, holding the door for him.

'Can I smoke a joint?'

'No. You cannot. And don't smoke joints. They stunt your growth.'

'But I need 'em. They cools me down.'

'Trust me, you are far too young to need cooling down, as you put it. Life is life, and you only have one, so make the most of it. Stop throwing it away.'

'Shit man, how old are you?' he complains.

I shut up. He doesn't want to hear and maybe one day he will be just as trapped as I am. And I am not about to tell him exactly how 'shit' that really is.

It is gone two by the time I get home. I have travelled in convoy with 40 tonne HGVs all the way back south feeling envious of the freedom they have. Hohne has left me a message saying I can have the next day off, which really does surprise me. Hohne isn't known for taking care of his personnel, unless it is a 'You are fired,' alongside a bullet to the brain. And Saturdays are his busiest times. We usually roll out of the gates before six in the morning and back in sometimes over twelve hours later. Me? I just kip when he is in meetings. I read a lot, too. Hohne usually ignores me while I drive, which is just the way I like it. He barks an instruction, rolls up the privacy screen, then makes and takes calls and does paperwork. It is, in many ways, a peaceful life. If only the threat of violence didn't rumble under the surface.

Chapter Three

I wake at ten and decide to take myself out for breakfast. There is a café where a little lady just might be having a coffee. It is such a long shot I am ashamed of myself, but I rarely have a Saturday free and I keep walking. When I arrive I find that the two pedestrian lanes near to the café, one that runs a couple shops away on the same side of the road, and one exactly opposite on the other side, are holding some kind of food or farmer's market. The sun has emerged and the lanes are full of vividly coloured canvas roofs and the myriad scents of burgers, hot dogs and curries. My stomach rumbles. I am bolting down a hot dog with curry sauce when I spot a head of glossy brown hair. My guts give a lurch, and there is nothing wrong with the hot dog. I polish off the last of my meal and lick my fingers enthusiastically. I begin to push through the hordes of bodies that exemplify London. Black, brown, coffee-coloured skins, freckled red-heads hem me in, and a dozen different accents and languages buzz around my ears. It is this multi-cultural side of London I really love, the residue of once being a huge empire. And it is her! I breathe in, and take a couple more steps. Then, amidst the hubbub and yells of stall-holders I whisper, 'Morning, little Evie,' close to her ear.

She gives a start, her huge brown eyes wide. 'Marco? What are you doing here?'

I stand upright, sheltering her from some over-keen lads carrying skateboards who are pushing through the throng. 'Hoping to get something to eat. How about you?'

She smiles, and my groin tightens. She is as lovely as I remember, the sweet curve of her cheek, her fabulous breasts not one iota less than in my memories of her. Something of what I am thinking must show in my eyes as a faint rose-pink brushes across her cheekbones.

'Likewise,' she says, and for a moment I am lost. What was the question?

I gather my wits and say, 'Fancy grabbing a bite to eat somewhere? I seem to have skipped breakfast.'

'Oh,' she stands there, staring up at me, and then she ducks her head, biting her bottom lip. As if I can see the thoughts running through her mind like newspaper banner headlines I know she is wondering to herself, should she be making friends with this big, scary Serb lorry driver. I swallow, feeling queasy.

'Marco, we have to get one thing straight. I am not 'little'. I am sturdy and if anything, rather plump.' She is frowning up at me.

At the word sturdy, all I can think is, good, so you will take my weight when I am on top of you, but that is hardly something I can say out loud in the middle of a street heaving with people. 'Evie,' I say, 'you only come up to my collar bone and your thighs are probably the width of my biceps.' Now her blush is bright red. Is she shy around men? She isn't particularly young, she has less years on her than I do, I think, but not that many. Was it the reference to her thighs or my biceps that has her blushing. I am tempted to give a quick flex of my arm and I think she guesses what I am thinking as she says, 'No.'

'No to brunch?' But she didn't mean that, so I am grinning even more.

Now she is even more flustered, 'Um, no. I'd like brunch.'

'Come on then,' I say, 'I know a decent Italian a little way along.' The crowd is still pushing us around in its eagerness to get at all the stalls, so I reach down and take her hand. She opens her mouth to protest, but closes it again and lets me lead her out of the throng.

As we reach the main street with its busses and taxies a girl enters into the market area right in front of me. She has a white blonde bob and is as cute as a pixie. She has tiny bones and comes about up to my sternum. She makes me think of delicate spun sugar, easy to break and liable to melt away into the air. I give the girl a thorough once over, thinking about Evie's word, 'sturdy'. I am not such a neanderthal that I don't realise it is a word she may use about herself but one if I used, I would likely be shown the door. Evie's hand is warm in mine, and I am holding her fast. I have her now, and I do not intend to let her go until she insists. I turn back to check she is ok as yet another boy carrying a skateboard swings around so the heavy board bangs into a woman's shoulder.

'Hey, sorry man,' the boy says. The woman glares at him. I stop and lean forward. 'Get that thing out of this crowd before I shove it down your throat sideways. And if you hit my lady with it, I will do it twice. Get me?'

The lad goes bright red and retreats out of the market. The woman smiles her thanks up at me, gives Evie a nod, and moves away. 'Your woman?' Evie asks.

'Well, at the moment,' I hedge, still gripping her hand.

'Really, after you eye up another woman while hanging onto me?'

I shrug. 'Yeah. She didn't come off too well. I prefer brown hair and brown eyes and a sharp tongue.' To my relief, little Evie laughs. When she tries to pull her hand away, I grip more firmly. 'Nope, you promised to come and eat with me.' I wait a beat to see if she complains.

'Let me go, and I will.' Her eyes are steady.

I let go, and can't hide my reluctance. 'I like holding your hand,' I tell her. She ignores me and heads off towards the Italian.

We don't make it to the Italian. A little French bistro I had never noticed is on the way and Evie's face lights up. 'Oh,' she sighs, 'hot chocolate, croissants and fancy pastries.' Evie has a sweet tooth, good to know.

I have black coffee, Americano, large. Since when did the Americans claim all large coffees as theirs? When I pose this question to Evie she gives me a, 'What planet do you come from look,' which I love, and it makes me grin. When she grin's back, the world feels exactly as it should be.

We talk about nothing, and it is easy. Then she begins to look at her watch. 'You have to go?' I ask. She nods, and my heart sinks. The rest of the afternoon and evening stretch long and lonely ahead of me, which is odd. For three years I haven't had anything to do in my free time and it hasn't bothered me one bit. I push my luck, 'Any chance you might go for a coffee on Wednesday afternoon?'

She looks at me, weighing me up. I gaze back. I can't change who I am. Either she accepts me, or I am too big, too brawny, too Serbian, whatever. She should come down on the negative. I am also caught up in criminality, though I try to hide that fact from myself. Somehow, watching Evie consider me, I am forced to face the fact that no decent woman should come within a mile of me. I am rotten fruit.

'I work, Monday to Friday, full time,' she says looking down into her empty cup. Then she looks up, frowning slightly. 'Wednesday, I was granted leave because,' she hesitates and her face goes stiff with control. I reach across and cover her hand with mine. 'It is ok,' I say, 'I get it. It was a one off. And I am sorry, really sorry, that you are still sad.'

'I am,' she says, frowning. 'I loved my Misty so much.'

Shit, she is going to cry and I can't comfort her here. I stand, my chair rocking back. I have no idea how much out bill is, so I throw a red fifty on the table and take her hand. 'Come on.' I tug her outside and pull her into a door embrasure. It is a solicitor's office entrance and clearly they don't work on Saturdays. I wrap Evie in my arms and she lets go and sobs into my chest. I stroke her back and hold her close and nuzzle her hair as her heart breaks. Yes, it was just a cat. But that little creature was Evie's friend, confidant, and comfort. Her grief is real, as was her love for her companion. Eventually she pulls away. My tee shirt is wet from her tears. I may act like a fool and never wash it.

'I am sorry. I can't believe how empty my flat, my life is, without her. She was so small really, but the hole she has left in my life is huge. Like, of planetary proportions.'

'Planetary, hey?' I smile down at her.

I am relieved when she smiles back up at me. I want to kiss her so badly my guts hurt as if I have been stabbed, but I pull back. 'I work Saturdays,' I say. 'Usually a twelve-hour day at least.'

'Seriously?'

'Yeah, serious as a heart attack. I have Sundays and most afternoons off, but work early mornings and often late into the night. Which is a nightmare, as I would love to see you again.'

'You have to drive around for all those hours?'

'My boss is a very rich man, and I also act as his bodyguard, which isn't hard. Men take one look at me and back away. Its why I work out so much. The idea is that they never take it into their minds to start anything.'

'So, how is it you are here today?'

Right then and there I decide never to lie to this woman. 'We had an attempted burglary last night. Four guys broke in. The police arrived and I didn't get to bed until six in the morning. My boss told me to take the day off. I think he has decided to work at home for once.' And that is the truth and pretty much everything I know.

'Oh, I see.'

Which leaves me thinking, exactly what does she see? 'Can I, see you again, perhaps on a Sunday?' It's the only day we both have free at the same time.

She licks her lips. 'No. My mother is in a nursing home in Felixs-towe, on the East coast. I go to see her every Sunday. She is frail, and I don't think she will last much longer, perhaps a year, perhaps less. My dad died when I was little, and she brought me up on her own. I won't lose my time with her for anyone.'

'May I drive you there? Only,' I remember, 'I don't have a car.' Every vehicle belongs to Hohne, and he is not a man you ask a favour of.

Evie begins to laugh. 'No, but thank you, oh car-less one. Having you beside me would distract me too much.'

That, I think, is a positive. 'Well, may I have your number?'

She looks at me, her head on her side. 'No, but you can give me yours. If I am ever free when I think you might be, I will be in touch. Perhaps.'

Ok, that is far better than an outright snub. I chant out my number and she taps it into her phone. Then she leaves me, with a smile as thanks for her chocolate. I watch her disappear into the crowd as if every hope on the planet has just walked away. She leaves a hole. A planetary sized hole. I head for the Italian. I will drown my sorrows in a huge bowl of pasta.

That evening I lie on my bed in the gloom as the light fades. I shove my hand down my boxers and do what I have been longing to do since the moment Evie walked away. I take myself in hand and grip hard. Behind my closed lids I see her face as she smiled up at me, and her moist, pink mouth. I nearly shoot my load simply thinking of her mouth so grip myself harder. Is she likely to ever go down on a man? The thought of her wrapping that sweet mouth around me makes me groan out loud. I spent the afternoon in the gym, trying to work off my lust, but nothing touched it. No matter how many kilos I hefted, nothing worked. I had finished off with a five-kilometre swim, more than two British miles, and that hadn't worked either. So here I am, comforting myself with the proverbial right hand, every lonely man's best friend. I give in and let her image swim through my mind. I imagine having her breasts in my hands, her thighs wrapped around me, being deep inside her warmth. My hand begins to pump and I come so hard I shake. I sink back into the mattress to discover that I have exploded so hard I have given myself a piercing headache. Well, that is a first. I sag, exhausted, and stroke myself gently, pulling the foreskin back, sliding my thumb over my tip, both soothing and rousing myself. And all the while my imaginary Evie floats through my mind. I rouse again, so easily when I think of her, and am close almost immediately. I pump my hand and explode again. I don't even have the energy to clean myself up. I pull up my shorts, pull the sheet over me, and sink into an exhausted sleep.

In the morning I can't shake off my depression. I am trapped in an illusory life. On the one hand, I do very little. I drive, clean the cars, clean my apartment, sometimes cook food, work out. I have no friends and no entertainments beside books, the tv and the radio. I am not lonely, because I don't allow myself to be. And then there is the reality. I work for a crook who has men killed without a second thought, is into every filthy way there is to make money, and who has me on a tight leash. And meeting little Evie has brought all of that into sharp focus. We have no future because I have no future. If Hohne learns I already care about her he might even use her to blackmail me further. I am thoroughly stuck.

I get up, drop down the stairs, park up the car, go back for breakfast and am standing, on duty, gun holstered, knife in its sheath, waiting for the man who owns me to appear. I stare straight into the middle distance and try to make my mind a blank. Every time Evie floats into my thoughts, I force her out. In the trees dotted artfully (so Hohne has told me) about the gardens a flock of large and shiny black birds cluster, rise in the air, settle again in the branches up above the noise of the unseen traffic. They mimic my thoughts. Black and unsettled. Hohne is dressed as usual in business attire. He keeps to the now fairly outmoded crisp shirt and tie look, and dresses me similarly. His own personal Ken. He is of average height and fairly slender, with dark hair that is silvering at the sides that he keeps immaculately groomed. He has a large hooked nose that gives his face character and his manners can be charming. He looks the perfect respectable business man.

We head out, sliding through traffic as only a limousine can, being held up in Stretham more than usual but then nosing onto the A205 through Dulwich until finally we are over the Thames and on the A14 towards Felixstowe. I wonder if Evie is there already and where in the town she might be. We are passing Marks Tey doing slightly below the speed limit when I spot a black BMW four cars behind. I drop my speed a little more and gradually, all three of the first cars pass me, but that black Beemer remains exactly three cars back. I hit the intercom. Hohne is staring at his phone, probably answering emails. He is undoubtedly an extraordinarily rich man, but I have to say this, he works for it.

'Mr Hohne,' I say, 'I believe we have a Police Interceptor behind us. Unmarked BMW.'

He looks up frowning, and meets my eyes in the driving mirror. 'Are we speeding?'

'Of course not, sir.' My voice is as bland as I can make it.

'Then ignore it.'

I allow my speed to edge back up to just under the limit again, but whatever goes on behind, whenever I look back, the black Beemer is there, always three or two cars behind. On a blank stretch of road he moves up behind and hits the blues and twos. At the sound of the siren I am aware of Hohne jerking upright in his seat. I pull over as safely as possible and wind down my window. A uniformed policeman walks over to stand by the window. I have already turned off the engine.

'Morning, sir.' He says, 'Your speed was somewhat erratic back there, have you been drinking?'

'No,' I say, 'in fact, I haven't touched alcohol in years.'

'I see.' I know from his expression he believes me to be a drunk; he cannot think of any other reason why a man might give up booze permanently. I wonder if he might congratulate me on staying sober? A small part of me wants to laugh, I don't suppose he can imagine the kind of fear that allows no loss of control, not even a little.

'Step out of the car, sir.' I do so. He is a big man, and we are eye to eye. 'This way, sir.' He leads me across and opens the back door of the black Beemer. It smells clean, I note.

'Do you have any documentation?' I hand him my UK driver's licence and details of the company insurance. As I sit there I feel a twist of panic. Am I properly insured to drive all of Hohne's vehicles? I have never actually asked him. 'HGV qualified I see, sir.' I nod. A small longing twists my guts. I liked driving lorries. I wish I still was.

He sits checking me out on what looks to me like an iPad, then gives me a nod. 'You are free to go, sir. Drive carefully.'

I return to Hohne and the car. As I pull away, leaning to check all of my mirrors properly, Hohne's voice comes over the intercom. 'Did they spot the gun?'

'I pushed it under the front seat as soon as I saw them.'

His only response is a snort. Whether of pleasure or displeasure, I have no idea. We continue on our way with no further apparent police presence until I slide the Merc along Trinity Avenue towards the part of Felixstowe docks where Hohne has his portacabin office. Felixstowe, on the East coast, is one of the largest container ports in Europe. His office is here is low key for him. If he is happy to pay to have an office in one of the most expensive and glossy office blocks in London, why have what is practically a shed here? It is just another of the Hohne conundrums I don't understand.

I park up in a 'lane' that runs between lines of portacabins, all like Hohne's. The area is quiet, which it usually is. Most of the cabins are used only when goods have arrived from one of the container ships; once dealt with, everyone goes elsewhere. Few are permanently staffed, but today feels even quieter than ever. In the background there is the constant noise of a huge port, of ships, cranes, shouts, clangs, all the signs of an efficient organised confusion. But here, between the identical green cabins, it is oddly silent. I step out of the car and look around, standing against Hohne's door to prevent him getting out. I take my pistol and hold it down by my leg, out of sight. Hohne sees, and gives me a nod. I stand back and he slides out, placing himself behind me. I walk to the half-open door of his office and push it open. These cabins are made of wood and plastic; they definitely would not stop a bullet. If anyone wanted to, they could fire at me and there would be nothing much to hinder the shot reaching me. Worse, it might collect fibres on the way and carry them into the wound.

I breathe in and move into the door opening. Six men are glaring at each other over a cheap desk. It is covered in dirty mugs, food wrappers and spills. Clearly they like their Micky D's. It looks as if there had been a row, but they had reached an impasse. One man, his back to us yells, 'And I say, I take my cut!'

'Do you,' says Hohne quietly, still mostly behind me.

The man swings around, 'Boss?' he blurts out.

'Get out,' says Hohne, 'and don't come back. I have no idea what is going on, but I do not like it.'

By now my gun has been spotted, and one lad, spotty and no more than twenty, goes white, which makes his acne look even worse. I smile at him, which makes him tremble. When did I turn into the bogy man? It seems that when we didn't turn up yesterday, word had got around that Hohne had been arrested and that the cops were likely to turn up at the cabin at any moment. My guess is that the good gentlemen in front of me were arguing about what they could get their hands on and who should get what. I step back, no one looks likely to do anything rash and this is Hohne's mess to sort out now.

I stay outside, but not in the car as usual. I work such long hours I often nap in the car, but not today. Instead I prowl around, keeping alert for anything unusual. Hohne eventually reappears and I open his door, wait until he is settled, then head for home. Some home, I think ruefully.

All the way back instead of concentrating on looking out for police I drive on automatic pilot, my mind on sweet Evie. I have been frozen for three years and had no hopes of having a future. One word from Hohne, and I have a bullet in my head, or worse. I thought I could do it. Just survive and wait until one day it is all over. The future was black hole I didn't particularly look into. Now, I feel as if I have an atom bomb in my groin and my mind is on Evie replay. Her sweet mouth, so pretty, the curve of her cheek, I am obsessed with the curve of her cheek, her brown eyes, so sad when I met her. I want to take the sorrow away and never let anything hurt or upset her ever again. I want to reach out and touch. I want to hold. I want more, so much more. And I have no idea if I will ever see her again. Worse, I know that I can only bring her sorrow and hurt. I am not good for her. Never will be. I am coming awake, and feeling bitter. I preferred it when I was frozen.

When we pull up at the house, I get out and open Hohne's door for him. When he is upright, I say,

'I have some questions.'

He glances up at me, then away. 'Do you.' But he doesn't stride off into the house.

'Why call the police. You have a nine-man rotating team inside, three always on duty, and me outside. Why couldn't we handle it ourselves?'

'Ourselves, hey, Marco? Becoming a team player are you?' I just look at him. He continues, 'You did well taking down the boy in the gardens.'

'He had a gun on him. What about the others?'

'We dealt with those. What did you do with the one the outside man had?'

'Ditched it in the Thames. I didn't know what crimes it had been used in and didn't want any of them coming back to us.'

He raises his eyebrows at the 'us'. Then he says, 'I knew who they were. Who sent them. I wanted to send a message. Calling the police seemed as good a way as broadcasting that they had failed as any.'

'Except that now they know my face and the car, probably all the cars, are on the APNR.' It is the automatic recognition system the police use. Every car that is fed into the APNR, if it goes past a police car, the police are automatically told that they should pay attention to it. I don't like being as visible as it seems I now am.

He breathes in audibly. 'Yes, well. I may not have considered all of the ramifications. But don't worry. The police won't bother you.'

With that he heads into the house. It is late, so I put the Merc away and gaze out over the other six vehicles. One is a purple cabriolet with bright yellow lines that mark the bottom of the bodywork all of the way around. Before my time, I have heard of a woman who lived with Hohne. Either he bought her the car, or she chose it, who knows? It is gaudy and screams, I have money and no taste. I wonder where the woman is now and shudder, glad I can't answer that question. His reassurance about the police is even more worrying. Who is he paying off for his quiet life?

I shower and change into a tee shirt and boxers for bed. I am exhausted. Yet I have done little today despite the late hour. I lay back and slide my hands under the covers and grip my shaft. Self-soothing they call it when babies suck their thumbs. I am slightly disgusted with myself, but only slightly. At thirty-five shouldn't I be beyond calming myself with my own hand? Shouldn't I at least have conned the skills sufficient to get a woman to do it for me? I slide my hand up and down and feel both the pleasure and the relaxation flow through me. I am with Evie at the French place, watching her close her eyes and lick her lips, saying, 'Only the French know how to make hot chocolate.' I wonder if I coated my shaft in chocolate would she lick it off? I let my fantasy drift. Would she let me coat her in honey? No, maple syrup. Easier to pour and I love the stuff. And then I remember the woman in Chechnya.

I still hadn't got a proper stubble on my chin. The guys had said she was clean and liked soldiers. I had been so nervous I was shaking. I'd had girls, but never paid before. We had been in her room, the lights low, and she had left me to go to the bathroom. When she came out she had been dressed as some kind of nurse, with a short fluffy dress, her tits hanging out, and a cap with a big red cross on. It was the syringe that fired my escape motor; it had been bloody huge. I'd got out of there as fast as I could, falling on my arse trying to tug my trousers up. I can still hear her calls, 'Baby, come back to Mumma.' Now, Evie playing dress up, that is an entirely different matter.

My hand moves faster and I groan as the feelings intensify. Evie fills my mind. I am fantasising about a woman I will probably never see again, and who should never have anything to do with me anyway. She has released me from my self-imposed prison, and I can't seem to clang the doors shut on my mind again. My chest constricts with grief at the same time as I come all over my stomach and hand. Truth is, I don't feel that much better. With a sigh I get up, get clean, and order myself to go to sleep.

As I do, before I slide into oblivion, I chew over the day. I have been seeing Hohne as omnipotent, but perhaps he isn't as clever and powerful as I thought? Calling the police was a foolish move, completely stupid, as far as I am concerned. It has put us all firmly on the police radar; being stopped by them today on the way to the port showed that. And that is what they were demonstrating to us, at a guess, though why make it so obvious? To rattle Hohne? My depression lifts a little. Is Hohne's empire at risk? Under attack? He has always seemed so clever and powerful. The way he has a guard of nine in the house, but only me on the outside, always seemed well thought-out to me. That way his business is well protected, but nothing on the outside seems excessive. I am far from the only driver regularly seen in a drive polishing limos in this area of London. And only I drive him, on the whole, so his large protection staff are fairly invisible. There is a back way through the garden that I have noticed does not have a camera, whereas nearly everywhere else is fully covered. The path and that outer gate are specifically outside the edge of the two cameras that cover that area.

The inside protection staff regularly go out that way and all have cars stashed nearby that never come onto the property. I am beginning to realise that I know more about Hohne that I realised. Exhaustion finally overtakes me as two more thoughts slide into my mind. Tonight was the first time I didn't call Hohne 'sir' every sentence, and he let it go. And secondly, if lovely Evie could go for a coffee on a Wednesday once, she might, just, do it twice. I know I am smiling. Life feels just a touch lighter.

Chapter Four

Two Saturdays later Hohne tells me he will not need me until late afternoon. I have a chance. Evie must live somewhere close to the café and where the pop-up farmer's market was. She hasn't rung or sent me a text. I am wishing I had pressed harder for her to give me her number, but why would she? I am just a large man she doesn't know who she struck up a conversation with on a couple of occasions. The comfort I gave her was nothing special. Anyone would have held her while she cried, it just happened to be me. She has probably never given me another thought.

I am down in the streets by eight, which is stupid. London doesn't start early on a Saturday morning. As the day ripens and the pedestrian traffic increases, I am beginning to call myself every kind of fool when I see her wandering along, peering into shop windows, passing the time of day with a man who bumps into her. I frown. Was that really an accident? I glance at my phone; it is nearly eleven. I am insane. What will she think if I go up to her? Will she be annoyed, nervous, irritated? I hang back and let people ebb and flow around me. Now I have seen her I don't know what to do. Perhaps it is my stillness in a flow of action that catches her eye, but she looks up and sees me. I am, perhaps, twenty metres away. Far enough that she can turn into a shop and ignore me. I stand still and listen to my heart beat. Then, she smiles, and begins to come towards me.

'I thought you worked Saturdays?' she greets me with.

'I am not needed until later today.' I can feel the muscles in my face stretching as I grin at her. Then I pause, 'I hoped I might bump into you again.'

She gives me a look that suggests she knows that I was looking for her. Women always know this stuff. All around us people are rushing by wearing back packs, carrying coffees, paper bags of sandwiches, groceries. The traffic noise is terrific, but we hardly notice it.

We wander along talking about nothing. The weather, if she has finished her grocery shopping, a drama she watched on tv. It is comfortable, but the streets are noisy now, so we turn into a side street and when I spot a pub bench, I nudge her gently and we sit. The air is moist here, the road cobbled, with silver metal barrels stacked up against the walls. No other customers have chosen to sit in this rather dank space. I drop my head and hunch my shoulders.

'Marco, are you ok?'

I don't lift my head at Evie's voice. I not sure what to do. I am sitting with my elbows on my knees, head and hands hanging. I sigh and sit up. Turning to her I tell the truth.

'I want to take your hand. I want to hold you in my arms. I ache to do that.' I shrug at the admission and gaze into her warm brown eyes. Her mouth falls slightly open, and she licks her lips and my eyes follow the movement. She has gone a little pink. I give a nod, and look away, across to the opposite wall. A small, warm hand comes to rest over my far larger one.

'Is that something terrible?' she asks softly.

The ache in my chest is acute. I wrap my hand around hers. 'I like you,' I say, 'I really like you. I love talking to you, hearing your take on life. I love watching how you react to the world. I think about you when you are not there, wondering what you are doing.'

I hear her take in a deep breath. 'Ok, so why do you make that sound like a really bad thing?'

Her hand is still wrapped in mine, and I look down and release it, but begin to play with her fingers, bending and straightening them gently. Then I look up and ask the million-dollar question.

'Will you come back to my apartment. Please.' I see her expression turn wary. 'This isn't a come-on.' I let her hand go. 'I won't touch you, I promise, but there is something I need to show you.'

She draws away slightly and I can see that she is unsure. I stand and step back, slightly away from her. The distance makes me feel chilled. Shit, have I gone too fast? Appeared to creepy?

'Will there be anyone else there? I mean, do you share with anyone?'

Hell, I sincerely hope not. My aim is to slip her in and out on the quiet. I have left Hohne at a hotel and I am not due to pick him up until six or seven. The indoor guards usually slope off when the house is empty. They may still be in the house but they will be using the gym, the cinema, the pool or just slobbing around in their private den on the third floor. It is rare that I ever see them out of doors. Evie is staring at me, waiting for an answer.

'No. It is a big house and my apartment is separate. There isn't usually anyone around at this time of day.' I pause. 'Does that make you feel safer or not?'

'Just how many girls have you snuck in mid-afternoon?'

I frown. 'You are the only girl I have ever invited back.' But why would she believe me?

Suddenly she seems to relax. Grinning now, she stands and reaches for my hand, tugging me along. 'Come on, you big lump, it is too noisy for conversation here, come and show me your lair.'

Heading back to my place we walk side-by-side, not touching but comfortable again. She had seen a new report about some green energy project that has got her excited and she tells me all about it. I half listen, more interested in her enthusiasm than the topic. At the rear gate she hesitates and gives me an uncertain look. I wait. Either she trusts me or she doesn't. The problem is, she shouldn't. Then she gives me a small nod, and I unlock the gate.

The path here runs straight into the fire escape that leads to my apartment. It used to be made permanently closed, but I was nervous. The lack of an escape route should the garage go up in flames worried me. We keep many containers of petrol in there, along with oil for the engines, paints for touching up, all of it flammable. And all of it immediately underneath where I sleep. So I forced the locks, then replaced them with my own. No one seems to have noticed. Again, as we step onto the grounds hidden from the house, I wonder how efficient and all-powerful Hohne is. Shouldn't he have noticed? It is a thought for another time.

We climb the metal stairs and I open the fire door into my apartment and then move back to allow Evie to enter. She gives me a glance, and then steps inside. I have left the gate below unlocked, and I know she noticed.

'Make yourself at home,' I say. I follow her in and set the coffee machine to begin working. 'Give me a moment, there may be cake.' I give her a grin and am pleased to see her smile back. She has placed her bag on the worksurface and is looking around. I leave by the main door that runs inside the building and leads out into the garden. Will she still be there when I return? I can only hope I am doing the right thing.

To my relief, only Carla the housekeeper is in the kitchen.

'Marco!' she calls, and comes to hug me. 'You bad boy. You have not been to see me for days.'

'I have a woman I am making coffee for. Is there any of your cake around?'

'Of course. You cannot have coffee without cake. Here, I have only this morning made a poppy seed cake. It is a Ukranian recipe I found in the newspaper. Take a piece, it is delicious. I make it with a special yogurt and everything with yogurt is good for you, no?'

I grin. The yogurt is clearly outweighed by the sugar content, but what the hell. Carla will never be persuaded that cake is not a health food, despite her girth. She steps closer and pinches my cheek. 'Who is this woman? Hey? You deserve a nice girl. She must be nice as she is the only woman you have ever bought here.'

I grab the cake and head out of the kitchen. 'Stop,' I say, 'You embarrass me,' but I am smiling.

I head back to the garage block and try to see it as Evie might. It is single storey with three double automatic doors and painted white. The floor above runs the whole length of the building but only the end with my apartment has windows, the rest of the wall is blank, the space being used for storage. It is topped with a red clay pantile roof. The gardeners have placed huge pots of some shrub or other along the front in between the doors and the red leaves of the plant echo the colour of the roof. It looks decidedly Mediterranean. If it wasn't for the man I work for, it would be an enviable lodging.

As I re-enter the apartment Evie says, 'Marco, this building alone could house a dozen or more families.' She turns slowly and looks across to the main house. I too turn to look. It is painted white, like the garage block, and has eight Georgian-style windows across the front with a shiny black front door that is double width. There are two round pale stone pillars supporting a huge porch and steps. Ten windows run across the first storey and are the same size as the lower ones. Above them are ten smaller windows under the eaves where the nine indoor security guys live.

'Most of it you can't see,' I say, as I put my hand on her lower back to edge her back away from the window. Evie shoots me a glance, but takes the hint and moves. The scent of coffee now fills the room, I find a couple of plates and cut off some of Carla's cake. 'Poppy seed cake?' I call over my back.

'Where did that come from?' Evie asks.

'Carla, the housekeeper. She runs the house, and loves to bake cakes and biscuits, but we have a chef who comes in for the proper meals. His assistant comes in at five-thirty and cooks and runs breakfast until ten, and then chef comes in at five and covers dinner until ten-thirty. Lunch, we are on our own.'

'Good heavens. And the food is part of the job? And this place? My, you have landed on your feet.'

I have my back to her, so I let my head drop and close my eyes. Then I take in a breath and carry the tray with coffee and cake over to the sofa. I leave one seat cushion between us and sit down. Evie's eyes are wide as she takes in my space. The double bed is over against the far wall, we are sitting in the middle area where my books and tv are, and the kitchen is against the outer wall. Everything is on view. Again, I try to see it through her eyes. I have nothing personal here. No family photos, no knick-knacks as reminders of happy times. The only items that might show my personal life are my books, but there are dozens of them on all sorts of subjects. Evie's mind is clearly whirring away. 'What did you mean, only part of the house is on view?'

'There is a double storey basement with cinema room, gym, twenty-five metre swimming pool, steam and sauna rooms and an absolutely enormous air-conditioned clothes storage area. There are nine security staff in the house and they have an area they call their den, where they hang out, watch tv and booze while off duty.' Her eyes are round. I smile. 'It isn't uncommon in London. As people cannot go sideways, they go up, or more often, down.'

'Good heavens.' She thinks for a while. 'What is your bosses name?'

'Hohne. Why do you ask?'

'Just wondered. As he has such a big house I thought he might be famous.' Evie has just lied to me. I drink my coffee and say nothing. Into the quiet she asks, 'Have you worked for him long?'

This, at least, I can answer truthfully. 'Three years.'

'What did you do before that?'

'Lorry driver. I enjoyed it. I worked for a Serbian transport company who moved goods and food stuffs all over Europe. I could be in Germany one day, Switzerland the next, and then Italy. They were really well run. I could drop a cargo off in one place, and pick up another and go somewhere else without having to go back to base.' I stare at the blank wall on the other side of the room above my bed. 'I suppose that was why I stayed single for so long.' I shrug. 'I never stayed in one place for more than a night or two. It wasn't a job for a family man.'

She is giving me a mischievous look. 'No women? Not ever?'

I give her a rueful half-smile. 'Yeah, now and then. There was always company if I wanted it.'

She doesn't say, I bet, but I can see her think it. I sigh. There were reasons why I remained unencumbered, but that tale isn't why I brought her here. I look across at her, and I can read her eyes, as no doubt she can read mine. The attraction fizzes in the air between us. The room is noisy with silence as we both admit without words what we both want. Her lips are plump and pink, her cheeks flushed with the palest of rose, and her pupils are dilated with longing. My groin is wound tight, my chest aches, and my arms long to haul her to me, roughly, and buy my face into her soft, silky hair. I swallow, and the sound seems to bounce off the walls.

'Have you noticed that I never wear jeans?' I ask. I can see her confusion as she shakes her head to say no. I raise my trouser leg to show the large knife buried safely in its sheath that is strapped to my calf. 'I only take it off at night, and then it goes under my pillow,' I say. Evie's confusion increases, so I nudge the drawer on my left open. It slides out on wonderfully smooth runners. I pick out my gun and swing it from the trigger guard with my little finger. 'My suits are made with extra stiffening on the left side so they never show the outline of my shoulder holster.'

I see her throat move as she swallows. 'Not just a driver, then,' she says softly.

'No.' I put the gun away and push my trouser leg down. I slump back into the sofa and close my eyes. She can easily go; the gate underneath the fire escape steps remains unlocked. I am not sure what to think as a warm hand slides into mine. I open my eyes.

'Why did you tell me, show me? All I have to do is walk to any police station and tell them what I have seen, and armed response will be here in minutes. You know that. The British police are pussy cats until weapons are on the scene, then they go hard core.'

'Yeah. I know. How else can I persuade you to go, and never come back? Because if you don't disappear, I am going to haunt that café and every street around there hunting for you. Perhaps not even to talk to you, perhaps just to see you. Don't you realise,' I close my eyes and give a sigh, then hold my thumb and index finger almost together, 'I am this close to becoming your stalker.'

'Stalkers are unwanted,' she says softly. Then she stands and I watch as she picks up her bag. I get to my feet and we stand like that, a couple of metres apart, not moving. Longing swirls in the air. I can see it in her eyes, in the now deep rose of her cheeks and throat, in the way she moistens her lips. A pulse is beating in my ears and I can almost smell the desire and lust and wanting as it roils around the room, sliding up the walls, swirling into clouds to come shifting around between us yet again. My groin aches and my chest is tight. 'I have to go,' she says, and turns to the door, her movements jerky and swift. 'Evie,' I say, but her response is as I expect, 'I have to think, Marco, I have to think.' I nod. 'Wait, just a moment.' I toss her a key on a ring. 'The code for the outer gate is 6, 7, 8, 9 and that key is for this fire door.' I hold her wide eyes, 'I don't care what time or day it is. If I am here, or if I ever come home and find you here, I shall be glad.' She drops her eyes,

'What it I appear and you are with a woman?' she asks. The question hurts.

We stand at the top of the metal fire escape and time ticks between us. Eventually I say quietly, 'No, Evie, no.' She glances up and then turns and goes down the steps. I follow, to see her to the gate. She knows that there is no other woman for me. I have ripped myself open for her. She knows that. At the gate she turns and says so softly I hardly hear, 'I am sorry, Marco.' Then she goes.

I run up the steps and rip off my clothes and replace them with my gym kit. I need to work out. Hard.

Nothing happens for two weeks. I drive Hohne, doze or read in the car while I wait for him, work out, keep the cars and my apartment spotless, and try to go back to the state of frozen limbo I was in before. Not thinking. Not feeling. And then I break. It is no good, I miss her. I want to see her. I want to smell that soft flowery scent that hangs around her. I ache for her. I am a bloody fool. But still, I go back to the café the following Wednesday and sit for hours reading on my phone and getting gut-sick of coffee. She doesn't come.

Chapter Five

I t is Saturday and we are heading towards Felixstowe container port once again. It covers a huge area and handles half of all UK container traffic. And if anyone tries to tell you that the customs and police know what is in all those containers, they are lying. The quay alone is at least two and a half kilometres long. It makes someone somewhere a massive profit though Hohne must make a whack from it as I have to drive him here at least once a month.

London to Felixstowe is a smooth route, but not once do I edge over the speed limit by the slightest amount. When we pass a thirty miles per hour sign, I am already doing twenty-nine. On the duel roads I never go above sixty as other cars fly by me. When I see a police car I glance across as if blandly curious. I also keep an eye out for more sleek black cars, often BMWs, who slide along with the traffic like sharks amongst minnows. The Interceptors. They are police in plain cars and these guys have all done advanced driving and are at times armed. The Brits really are an odd bunch. Most of the time they are armed with nothing more than a stick and a taser; but they know how to come in mob handed with serious firepower. One reason Hohne approves of me is that I have never once been pulled over by the authorities. I am a careful driver. Very careful. Always in control.

I started working for Hohne against my will, though that is another story. I had been working for him for a while, driving small vans and not asking about the contents, and we were in France when he asked me to drive him back to the UK. He kept me in place as his temporary driver and the days slid by. When I had been working for him for a month I asked to see him. He gave me a time and told me to appear in his study. It was my first visit and I can't remember if I was intimidated or not. It was all hunting prints, huge mahogany shelves packed with books, a massive matching desk with piles of papers and a computer; frankly, I thought it looked like Hollywood's take on an Englishman's study. Me, I'd have gone steel and glass, and it probably would have been a nightmare to keep looking good. So, I knocked exactly on the appointed hour and only entered after he had called out. I walked to his desk and he did that thing of fiddling with paperwork rather than look at me. Me? I stood and stared into the middle distance, hands loosely clasped behind my back, feet slightly apart. I was taking the piss really. Hohne liked to order people about and, in fact, was seriously rude about it. So I decided to stand as if I was a loyal foot soldier. I hadn't learned to be so afraid of him then. I knew he was a thug, I just didn't know the scope of his thuggery.

When he looked up he didn't speak, just raised an eyebrow. I knew he was trying to intimidate me. But really, he was fifty-ish and sat at a desk all day, and I was in my thirties at the time and my muscles had muscles even then. However, he has always considered me as dense as wood between the ears and I have always been happy to have him think that of me. I fell into this 'unthinking lacky' role by accident. By nature I don't say much. It is easy to believe if I don't speak I don't think, and then as now, I was happy to be underestimated. I was still learning about this world I am forced to inhabit.

I asked for three days leave and called him sir. He stared at me then said, 'No,' and went back to his paperwork. I stood for a moment wondering what to do, then turned to leave. As I took a step towards the door he said, 'What do you want it for?'

I turned back and looked at him keeping my face as blank as possible. 'For an advanced driving course.' I stayed where I was, now back to looking into the middle distance over his shoulder. He frowned, then asked 'Why?'

'If you are to consider keep me as driver and bodyguard, I need to be a good one,' I said.

'What kind of driving course?'

'They claim it is the same as the police advanced driving course.'

'Is it?'

'I am hoping it is.'

'What is it called?'

I give Hohne the details and he clicks away on his computer. 'I'll have it checked out. If their claim is correct, I will not only give you the time off, but pay for it.'

'Thank you, sir.'

As I leave he told my back, 'Any other courses appeal to you, come as see me first.'

As I was sick of saying 'sir', I just nodded my head and left.

There were other courses. I learnt a great deal. Hand to hand fighting, polishing my skills with hand-gun and knife. Hohne paid and I absorbed knowledge like the proverbial sponge.

This time there is no attempted coup at the Portacabin and the day slides by smoothly.

I go back to the café again the following Wednesday. It is late and I need to get back on duty, when she walks in. I am already standing, getting ready to move to the doorway. She is flushed and breathless and has clearly been running. 'I was too late, last week,' she says. 'I want to know more. I need to know more.'

'I have to go,' I say. I shake my head. 'I have to go to work.'

'Sunday morning,' she says, 'before I go to my mother's. Early.'

'You have the key, let yourself in. Whatever time it is.' I am so afraid that my voice sounds harsher than it should.

She gives a guilty glance around, 'What is one of the others shoots me as an intruder?' she hisses.

I nod. 'I promise, as long as you don't go into the kitchen for poppy seed cake, you will be safe.'

'Promise?'

Now I can finally smile, 'Yes, I promise.'

I move around her. I shall have to run, and run fast to get back in time. I set off at a jog. I shouldn't let her have anything to do with me, but I am sick of feeling dead, sick of being alone, and I want, just for once, to be selfish. But that doesn't ease the fear that I might be making a terrible mistake.

I get in on Sunday at four in the morning. I slide between the sheets too exhausted to do anything except pass out into a deep sleep. I have hardly slept since seeing Evie. My mind has been spinning with whether I am being an utter arsehole for putting her at risk, or am being right in reaching for some kind of human connection in this stupid, sterile, life of mine. What if she gets hurt? What if I don't reach out for her? Could I bear to go on not knowing if she might, just might, come to care for me? I tell myself repeatedly I am a bloody fool, but it doesn't stop me longing for her to take the risk.

I wake at six as the fire door opens. I sit up, immediately alert, to see a dark Evie-shape, enter the kitchen and close the door as softly as she can. I get out of bed and pad over to her in boxers and a tee. 'You came,' I say softly.

She stands in the half-light and looks up at me. 'I think I'd like a coffee,' she says, 'and perhaps a double whisky. Whisky is supposed to calm the nerves, isn't it?'

I am grinning. I can't help it. I go to put the coffee on, and she takes off her jacket and lays down her bag. Then she crosses to the drawer beside the sofa and pulls it open. She stares down at the gun, then crosses to the bed. When she is close enough to see the knife, she turns away and returns to sit on the sofa.

I put two coffees down on the side table, walk over to the knife and carry it back to sit one space along from her. I bend over and strap the sheath and the knife to my calf, then sit back and sip my coffee. 'What made you come?' I ask.

I can hear the long breath she draws in. 'Because I felt that you were not happy in the life you are living. You did not show me the gun to impress me with what a hard man you are, but to frighten me away. So, why not leave, Marco, if that is true? Why not just walk out and get another job?'

The big question. 'Because I am trapped. Like a fly in a web. When I wriggle, he just ties me tighter.'

'Hohne?'

'Yes.'

'Who is he really?'

'I don't know, but I doubt his real name is Hohne.'

'He is rich? I mean, super rich?'

'I imagine he is a billionaire, many times over.' I scratch my ear. What do I really know? He has made sure it is very little. A secretive man, our Mr Hohne.

'How did you come to work for him?'

I tilt my head backwards onto the sofa cushion and close my eyes. 'I grew up in both Serbia and England; long story. At eighteen, full of patriotism, I joined the Serbian army, but ended up with Russian officers fighting for them in the Second Chechen War. By twenty-four I was allowed to leave; my time was up. I had been a tank driver and had an HGV license so I went to work for an international haulage company. I loved it. I was free, on the road. No one ordering me to take morally dubious actions, like fire on a village full of women and children anymore. I could just drive, set my own timetable. I left at a certain time and, as long as I unloaded when I had been told to, the time in between was my own. I drove all over Europe including the UK until Brexit. Italy, Greece, Switzerland, Germany, France, everywhere. I saw places I had never even dreamed about. I could usually stay overnight and explore so it wasn't just the autobahns or motorways that

I saw. I ate food I had never known existed, spoke to people I could never have dreamed of meeting, and it suited me. The men with families took all the routine, regular routes, so I was free to take all the one-offs, or the really long journeys. And I was trusted. And I was worthy of that trust.

'Then, one day, I made an unusual trip into the UK. My company usually turned down those bookings. Getting into the UK after Brexit was bad enough with all the new paperwork, but getting out was a nightmare. Everything was difficult. The paperwork we had to complete kept changing, so we never knew if we would run into problems, even when we had done it all correctly as far as we could see. And although I could cross into France easily, all of the British drivers had to have their passports examined instead of just being waved through as in the past and, like it or not, we were always caught up in the lines of traffic. And because of the paperwork nightmare, we could never be sure what would be allowed across the UK border. So when I was told I was going into London, I was seriously surprised. I even questioned my management whether it was worth the hassle. That was when I should have smelt a rat. I could feel my line manager's unease, but I assumed that it was because the company would make a loss on the trip. But, in business, sometimes you take a loss to generate good-will, or other business. So I just shrugged, and got on with planning the trip.

'My load was to be machine parts, nothing surprising there and the paperwork looked good. I crossed into the UK with no problems, then when I stopped for breakfast at a service station a man came and sat beside me. He had a gun in his lap under the flap of his coat. He told me to keep eating and to stretch my meal out as long as possible. I was completely confused, and angry. I thought my load was being hijacked. I reached for the gun and twisted it out of his hand, then hit him in the side of the neck with a straight fingered jab. He slumped headfirst into the table. I didn't care who saw, I shoved my seat back and ran out towards where the lorries were parked, including mine. I got there in time to see about twenty people climbing out of the back and being loaded into vans. They were all young women. I was furious and ran forward shouting. A bullet landed at my feet spitting up tarmac. I stopped dead. Two men had guns pointed at me, one of which looked something like an M27. There was no way I could take on an automatic weapon like that. Then, the man I had left in the restaurant, appeared. He just reached for the gun and I gave it to him. I didn't see what else I could do.

'Then they all drove away. I knew I had been used, and was furious. I climbed into the back of the trailer and there was nothing there. Whatever they had lain on, or drank or peed in, had gone. There was no evidence at all. I had expected a filthy mess to be honest. I walked forward and opened one of the large cardboard containers. The inventory said machine parts, well, I guess they were. The first thing I saw was a washing machine drum. Shoved down beside it to stop it rattling was a broken computer screen. Every box was full of junk. I opened them all. I was parked right up in a far corner of the lorry park because this was where I had intended to sleep after my breakfast. On waste ground at the back of the lorry park was a smouldering bonfire of thin foam mattresses and cardboard. The smoke stank. I got out of there fast and drove for over an hour to another stop. Staying in the same place didn't seem a good idea. And that was where I made my really big mistake. I should have called the police, but I didn't know if I could trust them.

'Serbia had been waiting for years to join the EU; it was really important to us. Britain not only left, it took four expensive years to do it. The costs to the EU were enormous and all of that money could have gone into projects to improve life for everyone else. Our papers were full of how the UK was throwing away its membership and yet we needed to be members, and had to wait.

'Needed? For trade, you mean?'

I shook my head. 'Not just that, we wanted to be part of the EU because it is about the only organisation that can stand up to Russia. After Trump we didn't trust the US, China and India are somewhere else on the planet, so the EU was the most important friend we could make. It mattered. I wasn't sure what the UK stood for anymore, so I headed for home. I can't tell you how much I regret that decision.

'I got back to Serbia, walked into my main office, to find Hohne sitting at my boss's desk. The company was owned and run by two brothers, both in their fifties. The elder's face was a mass of bruising and the younger was sitting white faced, looking terrified. Hohne said,

'Made it back, did you?' and then demanded my passport. I looked to the two men I worked for and they both nodded. So I handed it over. He opened his jacket and put it in his pocket. I said something like, that's mine, and he said that now I worked for him, he would keep it. And then he dropped the bombshell, he now owned the company and I worked for him. I looked at the two brothers, men I respected and admired, decent men, family men, and said, 'No I don't,' and walked out.

'As far as I was concerned, I could get a replacement passport and I didn't need it to work in Serbia. I knew that I could drive anything, however big or heavy, and was a fair mechanic. I would easily find work. I headed out and began to walk to my parent's house. On the way my phone rang and a voice said, 'I suggest you reconsider.' I ended the call and carried on. I was half-way up my street when I realised that there was a crowd outside my family home. I shoved through to see my mother crouched on the ground with my younger brother's head cradled in her apron. She had her face turned to the sky and was wailing, it was an unearthly sound. There was a neat black hole in the centre of my brother's forehead, and his blood and brains were all over my mother. And then my phone rang. I put it to my ear automatically, I think I was in shock. The same voice said, 'Reconsidered yet?' I dropped the phone and putting my back to the wall I sank down to the ground. The nightmare had begun.'

'Does he still have your passport?'

Somehow that wasn't the question I thought she would ask. 'Yeah.' I open my eyes and turn to look at her. She is frowning and biting her bottom lip.

'And you want out?'

'More than you can imagine. But I am trapped.'

'Who have you told?'

'You.' I watch as she takes that in.

'Why me?'

Ah, now, I have no idea how to answer that, so I do what men since time began do, I shrug. And she gives a small laugh, which surprises me.

'I am honoured. And there has to be a way out, there just has to be.'

Is she speaking as someone who wants to be my friend, or are we on the same page? I breathe in, not sure what to say or do now. She is really chewing that bottom lip. I slide my thumb over it to stop her doing herself an injury. She freezes, and her eyes go dark, and I find that I too am afraid to move. Just that small touch has ignited me and, unless she is a total innocent, she knows how I feel about her. And then she smiles.

'Two minds are always better than one. There is more, I am sure, but you have given me enough to absorb for now. I don't think I am strong enough to hear what else he has put you through. There will be a way out of this, I know there is.'

And something rare creeps into me. Hope. But how can this small, lovely woman, help a big lump like me?

'Evie, it's not your problem, I only told you so that you knew what you were getting into if we became friends.'

Her grin widens. She knows full well I want more than friendship, but at least now she will never be able to accuse me of keeping stuff back from her.

She stands, 'I have to go. I am never sure if Mum will recognise me, so I like to spend as much time with her as I can. A couple of weeks ago I had to go down on a different day, a Wednesday, (she shoots me a look, does she wonder if I waited for her in the café?) and I ran her to the hospital. Last Sunday she told me that a lovely lady had taken her for her appointment.'

'Doesn't that break your heart?' I wonder how my beloved parents are doing without me? They must think that I simply deserted them. I call, but lie about what I am doing. And, of course, I cannot go home.

'More than I can say, but at least I know that one day a week she has company sitting beside her. Often, I read a book, but she is close, and these days that is all I can have. The person inside is gone.'

On instinct, I pull her into my arms. I want to comfort her, to shield her from the agony of losing a loved mother in such a slow disheartening way. Would my father tell me if my mother was going this way? Sliding into dementia?

Evie feels stiff in my arms, but as I go to move away, she melts into me and wraps her arms around me. I hold her close, rubbing up my hand up and down her back. She feels every bit as good as I imagined. I bury my face into her hair and breathe in her scent. She smells like everything that is good in life. When she pulls away her eyes are damp. I step back, not wanting to give her more than she is ready for, but she smiles up at me.

'Thank you,' she says softly, 'I needed that.'

I nod, 'I'll walk you to the gate. You have your key?' I grab a tee shirt and pull it on, and then zip and button my trousers fully closed. When I glance up, her eyes are locked on my hands. I give her a wicked grin and she grins back, then goes red, laughs a little, and looks away. I shove my feet into trainers and we head to the door. The way she was watching me tells me all I need to know. As we step out onto the fire escape landing I whisper in her ear,

'Do you wear a thong?'

She gives me a wicked grin and answers just as softly. 'Tried one once, found it uncomfortable. But then, I had no reason to persevere, did I? Why do you want to know?' Her expression is pure enticement.

'So I can imagine what is beneath your clothes when I think of you.' I tell her softly, burying my face into her luscious hair and letting my words filter through.

'Well, at present always plain white or black bikini pants.' Her face as she looks up into mine is pure wickedness.

'Sheesh,' I gasp, and swallow. With a quick spin, she is dropping down the fire escape stairs. I stand for a moment, my mouth wide trying to catch enough air to breathe. But my heart is flying. My judgement, for the first time in a long while, is spot on. Evie will be mine. Not yet, but soon. I chase after her, laughter bubbling inside.

At the gate I sober. 'Hey, what are you driving?' I don't like the idea of her going that route in something unroadworthy. She tips her head to one side,

'Worried about me?'

'Yeah, a bit.' Should I admit just how much I want to make sure she is safe? Always, all the time? She might not like that idea. Am I too raw for her?

She reaches up and slides a soft, warm hand behind my neck. My heart stutters and I sort of freeze. I don't want to mess this up. She pulls me down for a soft kiss, the merest touch of lips. 'Stop worrying; I hire a car. It is going to be delivered at my place in about twenty minutes, so I have to run. It is all double yellow lines and I don't want a ticket.'

I swallow. Every fibre of me wants to crush her to me but I was, once, a soldier. I can control myself. Can't I? With a flick of her fingers she is off, hastening down the street away from me. She leaves me standing there, utterly enslaved. But I can't keep the grin off my face as I run back up the stairs to my place. She will be back. I know it. But shit, I still don't have her number.

It is nine thirty the next Wednesday morning. I open my door and the hairs on the back of my neck go up. Someone is in my apartment. I step forward, my hand already on my gun and Evie steps forward.

'I let myself in,' she says. 'I hope that is alright. I have the day off work.'

My jacket is thrown off and I have her in my arms in an instant. This time I don't hesitate, I kiss her with intent, devouring her mouth. When I finally release her she looks up at me, her face with that flush I love and wish to deepen, her eyes wide, her tongue licking her swollen and damp lips.

'Oh,' she says.

'I missed you.' I complain. I bury my face into the side of her neck and gnaw lightly.

'Do you always growl when you don't get what you want?'

I can't help but grin down at her. Growl? Me? Yeah, well perhaps. 'Too fast?' She places the flat of her palms on me and I step back. 'Sorry,' I say.

'Sorry for wanting me? Or sorry for kissing me the instant you saw me?'

'Both?' I shrug, not sure if I have messed up.

'Marco, I loved your kiss, and I am absolutely beyond flattered that you want me. But you have hit me with some seriously heavy stuff. We need to talk first.'

Talk? I want to rip her clothes off and sink into her, as deep as I can plunge. I have already scoped out her clothes, and there are too many of them and far too many buttons and zips. As she looks up at my face I complain. 'I still don't have your number and it has been hell hoping that you would come back.'

She smiles up at me and pats me with her palms. 'Poor Beast, it wasn't deliberate. Give me your phone and at least next time I can ask permission to arrive.'

'You don't ever have to ask,' I tell her, and mean it. Then, 'Coffee?'

'I'd like tea, if you have it. And pass me your phone.' My smile deepens, going down to the soles of my boots. I unlock my phone and pass it to her. She is bossing me about and shows no fear of me. I fancy her even more.

First I stow my gun and knife. I don't want weapons hanging off me if we are going to talk. Or do anything else. 'Beast?' I ask as I cross to the kitchen area and reach for mugs and teabags, 'What did I do to deserve that?'

'I don't know, it just seems to fit. You are so big and wonderfully strong,' I look over my shoulder to see her teasing expression, 'yet you are trapped here, unable to leave.' I make the tea and carry it over to the side table and set it beside where she is curled up on the sofa.

'Did you know,' she continues, 'that some countries sell their passports?'

'What do you mean?' I didn't think such a thing was possible. 'Surely you have to be born in a country to request a passport? I mean, I know about dual citizenship such as when a Brit is born in the US and can have a passport from both, but it still depends on, I don't know, who you are.'

'Not any more, I have been doing research. Wealthy countries like the UK, USA and Canada have been selling special visas to rich people since the 1980s.'

'So, if you are rich, you can buy citizenship?'

'It gets better. You can buy a passport from all sorts of countries if you simply have enough money. St Lucia, for example. Do you fancy living in the sun for the rest of your life? Or, Malta, perhaps or if you have more money, how about Austria? To be honest, there are loads of sellers.'

'I can't believe this.'

'I'm not making it up.' Evie looks a little indignant.

'No, Princess, I don't doubt you, it is just that I mention one problem I have, no passport, and you come back with a solution. All I need is a load of money.'

'Well, we can talk about that. Could we steal it from Hohne?'

The cheek of it causes me to throw back my head and laugh. 'You are wonderful, you know? Absolutely the best thing that has ever happened to me.' They idea of robbing Hohne is great, until you think about who he is and what the repercussions would be. Until we can escape off planet, it is not an option. But I love that she is thinking about it. She is sipping her tea and looks at me. 'It has been a long week,' she says, and sighs. I long to knead every tight muscle in her body, and ease one of mine, but I stay one sofa cushion away and drink the coffee I made for myself. I might be a Beast, but I can try to be a well-behaved one.

'Marco,' she says, 'how is it that your English is so good? I mean, you have only the slightest accent that give away that it isn't your first language, and sometimes your sentence construction indicates it,' she adds as an afterthought.

My sentence construction? I hide my face behind my coffee cup. What the hell does that mean? Clearly, my Evie has brains as well as beauty. It makes me a little unsure of myself. At heart, I am a lorry driver. Not exactly a captain of industry.

'Because of my aunt,' I say. At least I can answer this. 'Her husband was a lawyer, a barrister, I think. British. He was working in Serbia for the UN, probably because of the Serbian Bosnian conflict that had by then ended. My mother is a beautiful woman, but her sister was stunningly lovely. He swept her off her feet and across the continent to the UK. When I was five, she was visiting and someone firebombed our local school. I had an older brother who was ten and there was another school he could go to, but there were no school places for little ones like me, and wouldn't be for another year.'

'Firebombed?'

I nod. 'Our area was pretty lawless, but it was our home, and where else would we go? My parents still live there.' The truth was, crime sat over everything, like a layer of dust touching down on every surface.

'So, what happened?'

'My aunt didn't have any children and contacted her husband, my uncle. He pulled some strings and I was given permission to leave the country and enter Britain. I went to live with her and attended the local school. I hated it. I missed my mother terribly, and my elder brother despite the fact that we fought all the time. I didn't understand the language and despite my aunt's love, was miserable. There was a teacher, a Mrs Willis. She took me under her wing and gave up her own time to teach me some of the words I needed to know.'

'You remember her name?'

'Yeah. Why would I forget her? I remember her smell too, but not her face, oddly enough. Anyway, I picked it up fast and soon was playing football and chase with the other kids.'

'Did you ever go home?'

'Yeah, but not for two years. I missed my mother the most.'

'You sound as if you still care for her.'

'My Mama? She is a wonderful woman and I love her to bits.'

Evie begins to laugh softly. 'Oh, Marco. What you have just done is, to me, so un-English.'

'What?'

'You placed your hand over your heart and swore devotion to your mum. I simply can't imagine any other man I know doing that. It was very,' she pauses, 'Serbian.'

I am not sure whether to be offended or not. She reaches across and places her hand on my thigh for reassurance. I look at her and she whips her hand away, her mouth pursed and her eyes dancing with mischief. I feel a smile wipe across my face. I might not have got her into my bed, but she is here, and it is good. 'So, I can't believe that two years as a child made you so fluent,' she continues.

I sigh, 'No. In 2003 there was a political revolt in Serbia, life became dangerous in our area. My elder brother had already immigrated into Germany and was learning how to be train driver. They were short of them,' I shrug. 'He has since married a German girl and they have two children whom none of us have met. Nor have we met her. He severed all contact with us years ago. Where we live,' I hesitate, 'it is not a good area, you know?' And why would he want to acknowledge a brother who works for an evil man like Hohne? But I have enough sense not to say that, though I feel it deeply. He is ashamed of all of us, but I deserve it. Mama and Tata, no. 'I was fifteen when the revolt happened, so once more I came to school to England. I stayed for three years. This time I had two brothers to miss.'

'It sounds as though schooling for you was important to your mother and father.'

I shrug. 'Me, I didn't care so much, but again, the teachers really pushed us and encouraged us to learn. And I enjoyed it. They wanted me to go to university but by the time I was 18 I wanted to go home. Not that I stayed, I joined the army. My parents were horrified. They wanted a good life for me, to have choices in my future other than crime or factory work. I have completely failed them.' I look down at my hands, and the shame that lives inside washes through me. Evie moves across to settle closer to me and takes my hand. I look at her, and I do not see shame, I see kindness. 'You have beautiful eyes,' I tell her. She smiles.

'As do you.'

'So there is one bit of my you approve of,' I tease.

'Ah Marco, I suspect that there is a lot of you I approve of,' she is smiling at me and it is like sitting in front of a warm fire.

'Are you going to kiss me?' I tease again.

She shakes her head and moves back again, but she is smiling widely. 'Maybe. If you are a good Beast.'

'I am sick of me. What about you?'

'Oh, I am very ordinary. I loved school. I was the class swot, then at university I was the geek, the nerd. Always with my head in a book. Did every assignment, passed every exam with flying colours, and was completely uncomfortable around people. I think going to an all-girls school did that. I was horribly teased, bullied really, by the others for being so studious and boys seemed an alien species I never came into contact with. I made some really close girl-friends at uni, and I think it was only then that I began to trust people to like me.' She gives a small laugh, 'I had, perhaps still have, serious insecurity issues.'

'Yet you trust me? A man you call Beast.'

She looks remorseful, 'Oh Marco, I won't call you it again. It wasn't meant to put you down. It is just that you are so beautiful and so trapped.'

I lean across towards her. 'It is you who is beautiful.'

'No doubt,' she says crisply, 'let's go for a walk. Is that possible?'

I shrug. I can like walking. When it is with Evie. 'Hyde Park or Green Park? Both are close.'

'Hyde Park, let's walk along the Serpentine.'

I go and fetch my knife, haul up my trouser leg, and strap it on again. If I may accidently cut Evie with it I won't wear it, but if bed is not an option, I prefer to have it near.

'Do you really need to wear that?'

I glance up at her. 'While I work for Hohne, yes. He has many enemies. One day, I'd like to throw it far out to sea where it will never be found.' But I know, that is unlikely to happen. My days are numbered; I am a marked man. But for the moment I have hours of free time and a beautiful woman by my side.

We head out to the park, which is only a few streets away. What I can never get used to is how green London is. If you go up high and look over the city there are trees everywhere. The town I grew up in Serbia was a kind of grey-brown colour, and nothing grew in our local streets. Serbia is a beautiful country, but our patch wasn't.

Evie is walking a definite distance from me, and I do not try to close the gap. As we leave the gate she says,

'What if we met one of the security men?'

'They move around mostly when it is dark. Times like now, when I have delivered Hohne and he is somewhere safe, they catch some sleep or eat or workout. They aren't particularly visible in the daytime. If the locals, or the police, knew that he had a private force of nine men in the house, it would call attention to him. Me? I cause no surprise. That a rich man has a driver who can double as a body guard is quite normal around here where the extremely rich make their homes. I meet other men just like me, who waste their time polishing clean limos and wait. I do a lot of waiting.'

'Marco, what does go on?'

'Honest truth is, I am not sure. Drugs, I suppose. I take him to Felixstowe to the port regularly, but I have never actually seen proof of anything. There is probably other stuff, but I am kept away from it. The guys in the house are the ones who go out and act for Hohne. I just keep him safe.'

'Why does he trust you?' I can see her bewilderment.

'Because he shot my brother in the head, and if I step out of line, he will do the same to my mother. After that, my father.' I shrug and smile. It is as it is. I have given up worrying. As the philosopher's say, now is all there is.

She frowns, then turns and strides away. I hasten a little, catch up, and walk beside her.

'Did you grow up in Felixstowe?' I ask.

'I did. It is an odd place, a mixture of run-down and up-coming. Ipswich is our main town for the major shops. The beach is mostly pebbles, so it is tricky to find areas where sandcastles are possible. As a child, I never ran on the beach in bare feet, it would hurt too much, so going to the seaside meant plastic shoes for me.' The memory makes her smile.

'What happened to your father?'

'He died when I was ten. Cancer. It was discovered too late for treatment so the three of us went to Barbados. He died two weeks after we got back, but it was a wonderful trip. He seemed so well, and then we returned and the end began. Mum was devastated. She talks to him all the time now her mind has gone.'

I frown, chewing that over. Does that hurt her? That her mother talks to her invisible father but not to her? But I don't know how to ask the question.

Hyde Park is, as always, busy in parts. We are striding along a path when two pretty girls come walking towards us; not my type. Too much make-up and self-awareness for my taste. All I do is glance at them to ensure we don't walk into them. After they had gone passed, Evie takes my hand. I look down at her. She gives me a sideways glance.

'I saw the way they looked at you,' she says, looking ahead again. 'For this morning, you are mine.' Now I really am grinning. I feel like that cat that got the cream. She slides me another sideways glance. 'Huh,' she says, 'you look entirely too pleased with yourself.' Now we are both grinning.

We slow our pace when we reach the path alongside the Serpentine. There is a van and we stop for cones piled high with whipped vanilla ice cream and flaky chocolate. We talk about nothing, just chatting and content to be out when the weather is pleasant and to be in each other's company. I am completely content.

We strike across the depth of Hyde Park and find our way to Green

Park, then across to Pall Mall before walking through St James's Park, before ambling back towards Onslow Gardens.

'Where do you live?' I ask. I watch her face as she bites her bottom lip. Then she slides her hand into my pocket, removes my phone and gives it to me to open. Then she types the address into the Notes. She closes the phone without showing me what she has written, and returns it to me. 'How about I walk you home?' I ask.

She stands watching me, then says, 'Not yet. Marco, I know that you are not a fourteen-year-old schoolboy who wants to get his hand inside my bra. I know what you want. But I need time.' I have no idea what she really means by this. She finishes with, 'I do really like you.'

This sounds a lot like 'it is not you, it's me', to me. I swallow. Today has been a gift. A beautiful gift. I tell myself I must not ask for more. I don't deserve it. She gives me a small smile, 'Thank you for today.' And then she is gone, walking away from me. I head back to the place that is my home. I have a Mercedes to polish and a load of weights to throw around.

That night, when my phone pings, it is Evie. I read her message, just 'Good night'. I smile and text her back, 'I miss you,' I say, but there is no response. Hohne keeps me out, driving here there and everywhere until it is almost dawn. For the first time I begin to memorise all of the buildings he enters, I mean, really memorise. The addresses, whether he goes up a level, who is there to meet him, what they look like. I think, up to now, I haven't wanted to know, but meeting Evie has changed all that. She seems to believe in me, if only a little. It is time I paid attention and gathered evidence. Not to write down, I am not stupid, but in my head. Some of the contentment I felt wandering around with Evie today returns.

Chapter Six

Evie sends me a text message a few days later. She wants to
know if I always have Wednesday afternoons free? I say yes,
from about ten until six, most weeks. It is true, I usually drop
Hohne off at his office every Wednesday morning. His office is inside a
tower block called 22 Bishopsgate, or sometimes, because it is so prestigious, simply 22. When it was built it was the second highest block in
London, after The Shard, but it has probably been overtaken by now. I
have been told it is the most expensive office space in the City and is
south of the river, and I have learnt from living in London the snob
appeal of being 'south'. It stands at the end of Threadneedle Street,
where the Bank of England is and its base is buried in the huddle of
ancient lanes that make up this area that is full of elegant and historical
stone buildings. Building it must have been fun. There is nothing easy
about this location which is a tangle of lanes nestled deep in the old
city.

The list of companies that are inside are all huge international
companies, so I am not sure how Hohne fits into all this. For the privi-
leged who work there, there is a gym, cafés and restaurants and no
doubt loads of other goodies. As a mere driver I am not allowed to

venture in without permission, no doubt in triplicate. The bit that always makes me think, is that outside, where I stop to deliver him to this airy castle in the clouds, is on double red lines. When I first began driving in London I had no idea what they meant. Double yellow lines painted on the road next to the kerb are everywhere, and are regularly abused by Londoners. They mean don't park, and we will slap a fine on you if we spot you. But the double red ones are a London speciality and mark out the routes through London that are essential for the functioning of the capital. In other words, don't even think about pausing to drop someone off, or we will come down on you like a ton of bricks. And every morning, I park on double reds right outside 22 Bishopsgate and get out and walk around and open the door for Hohne. And after he has begun to walk the half dozen steps to the main door, I reverse the procedure. And this space is right between two sets of traffic lights. And is on camera. Probably more than one camera. Yet, as far as I am aware, we do this regularly without any official censure. So who exactly, does Hohne have in his pocket?

When I have left him it is usually a little before nine; I work my way back through the traffic to the house. Wipe down the car so it is ready for its next journey and by ten I am usually free. At seven in the morning the following Wednesday she sends me a text. I reply saying that yes, I can meet her outside the gate at ten thirty. I am not sure how I drive Hohne to his office at 22 Bishopsgate that morning because I see nothing, I am completely on auto-pilot. If anyone wants to hijack Hohne, today would definitely be the day.

I am early, of course. I have not been texting Evie except to reply to her; I am too afraid of frightening her off. Every night she wishes me goodnight, and every morning I wish her good morning. Nothing more. I am a fish watching the bait and wondering if it will taste nice, or if it will haul me into the air to suffocate. Evie arrives with a huge grin as if she is glad to see me and we fall into walking together naturally. No welcome kiss. Oh well. I am so hungry for her company it doesn't matter. Much.

We wander around Covent Garden and I point out where the stall

Meg Barber

is every Tuesday where I buy books second-hand. She begins to tell me about a book she has read recently that excites her. It is science fiction and that worries me. Yes, I read English well, but sometimes it loses me and following a complex sci-fi plot could well be beyond me. I decide then and there to find one and have a go.

We find some lunch at a Mexican place and then wander into a small park to let the food settle. It is quiet here, and then I realise that we are in a graveyard. The tall grey wall to my right is the side of a church. This is what I love about London. That church might have been built in 1450, and here it is, still simply by its presence creating an oasis of calm. Out of nowhere Evie asks,

'Marco, do you want to kiss me?'

What do I say? I'd rather we were in my bed right now? So I go for the simplest truth. 'Yes.'

She looks up at me, her eyes huge and sad. 'I am not very good with men, I mean, romantically.' She means sexually, of course. So I say nothing. She looks down at her hands and I see her throat move as she swallows. I want to take her hand to reassure her that whatever she says is alright, but instead clench them on my thighs to keep them still. 'I told you I was bullied at school, and that boys were a complete mystery to me.' I want to interrupt and tell her that boys are often simple. They think with their dicks. Understand that and you understand pretty much everything, but I remain silent. 'I wore glasses with huge thick lenses; I was almost blind. I had to wear them through most of uni, and then I spent every penny I had including an overdraft at an iniquitous rate, and paid for a private operation.'

'On your eyes?' I blurt out. She has beautiful eyes, and the thought of someone cutting into them with a knife horrifies me.

She nods. 'I have to wear glasses in the evenings, I can usually get to seven or eight, and then my eyes get tired and the glasses help. But basically, the operation transformed my life. I began to make girl-friends, wear more fashionable clothes, practise a little flirting. And I was in my own quiet way, happy. I was never going to be that drunken girl dancing on the table, but hey, I loved my studies and for the first time in

62

ages, was content. I did a four-year degree and came out with a good result and was offered a job immediately. I could have waited for a better offer with a bigger company, but I was deep in debt and was relieved to think that I could now begin to pay it off.

'Lucas hit on me as I was walking from the Tube station to work one morning. He bumped into me, began chatting, asked me to meet him for coffee after work. I was amazed. He was quite tall, slender and dark-haired, and clearly interested in me. I met up with him and thought him wonderful. Two months later I moved into his flat, and a year later we got married.'

I sit back on the bench, winded. Little Evie is married. And, to bang a final nail in my coffin, she likes slender dark men. Not, clearly, big burly ones. 'Are you still married?' I have to ask. I don't care in a way, but in another it feels the most important question I have every asked. I wonder if Hohne would do me a favour and knock him off? I could offer to work without pay for a year?

'Marco, what are you thinking?'

'How to look up how long I would get for murder in this country,' but I grin at her.

'Good thought,' she says with a grin, 'but no need. We have been divorced for nearly three years.'

'But he has, what, made you nervous of men?'

She doesn't say anything for a while then admits. 'I changed my name to Eve Scott by deed poll.'

'Why?' The word explodes out of me and I chant, control, control.

'Despite the divorce he wouldn't leave me alone. He would turn up banging on my door demanding I let him in. He would be outside work when I left and follow me to the Tube. It was constant.' She gives a huge sigh. 'It wasn't until I left him I realised that in four years I had lost all my confidence, given up all of my few precious friendships, stopped doing anything but work and clean his apartment. He owned me. And after I left, it was clear that he wanted to keep on owning me.'

'What happened?'

'I went to the police to request a restraining order to keep him away

63

from me, but they told me he wasn't doing anything that I could really complain about. Basically, I had no evidence that he had beaten me up so they were not interested. And I don't blame them really, they have to deal with all of society's ills, not only crime. I had seen a lawyer about the chances of obtaining a restraining order so I went back and asked how to disappear. She arranged for me to legally change my name, helped me write a new CV so I could look for a job, and acted as a referee to explain to any new employer why all my qualifications were in a different name. She was great. Despite that, none of the big companies would look at me, and I was only offered one job, so I took it. They know about my past and have promised never to reveal my previous name.'

'What's his name?'

Evie looks at me. 'No Marco, I don't need a knight in shining armour.'

I am slightly offended. But only slightly. I tell her, 'Despite what you think you see when you look at me, I am only a simple lorry driver who would like to go home to see his Mama and Tata. The smile Evie gives me suggests that she is not convinced. I shrug and breathe in deep. 'You are telling me no more kisses and that you just want to be friends.'

'I think I am.' She is not looking at me.

'I accept,' I say. 'But I would like some trust. Will you show me where you live? I'd like to know I can put a Christmas card through your door.'

Evie stares at me for a long moment, then says. 'Would you like a coffee at my place. As my friend?'

How she thinks that is going to work I don't know. She bumps into me when we walk together, reaches out to tap me unselfconsciously, and her eyes darken when I look at her. Whether she is aware of it or not, she trusts me physically and is comfortable in my company. Most importantly, she is not afraid of me. And her body wants me, even if her mind remains doubtful. I can wait. When we stand, I feel smug.

Her apartment is smaller than mine. We sit on her sofa and drink bad coffee and discuss books that we have read and heaven only knows what else, but suddenly it is time I got back to work. As I stand to leave she says, 'Next Wednesday?' I stare at her, bewildered. She sees my uncertainty and blushes a deep pink. 'I have told my bosses that I have to go to Felixstowe to take my mother to hospital appointments for the next few weeks, and that I will work Saturdays instead. They have agreed.'

'So you have every Wednesday off?'

All she does is nod. I am jubilant. I pull her into my arms and kiss her with all the joy I feel. She likes me. And who says a grown man cannot be a fourteen-year-old boy at times. She fits perfectly in my embrace. I feel her weight increase on my arm as she relaxes into the kiss. She is sunshine and hope all rolled together. Her arousal rises parallel to mine. 'You did this deliberately, didn't you?' I challenge, 'You know I have to be back at work in a matter of minutes.' She gives a wicked little nod. I slide my hand up her jumper and cup the weight of her left breast in my right palm and she gasps, and not with horror. 'You will be mine one day,' I breathe against her mouth, 'but not until you are ready. This is a penalty for being mean to me.' I squeeze her breast gently. She gazes back with glazed eyes and plump wet lips. 'Tormentor,' I whisper, and leave before I forget my own name and toss her onto her bed.

As I jog back through the streets I am wondering how I can find out the ex-husband's name. It is a question that haunts me for days. I have never been interested in social media, but I create a false id and haunt every site I can find for hours at a time. I get backache and discover that there are some very strange people around. Some of it makes me feel grubby, and I am getting nowhere. In the end, I decide to ask Evie outright. I send her text. It is the longest text I have ever sent, and I assume that she will ignore it, as she has always done. But a name comes back, Lucas Wainwright.

That sends me into a spin. Why would she tell me? How much am I being used? If so, I am going at a cheap price; a few kisses and one grope. I know I am feeling bitter and uncertain and only action will help, so I stalk Wainwright online, now I have learned how.

My new thoughts take me back to where I was before I met her. I tell myself that I don't believe anyone. Not even pretty, sweet, little Evie. In fact, I have always been inclined to believe women less in general. Even men with rows of certificates on their walls can be as dumb as pig shit; women, however, read people. They follow nuances and emotional flows. I think it is called 'emotional intelligence'. Men lie to you because they are stupid and arrogant so believe that you will swallow their tales; women 'learn' you, then feed you a lie that you are far more likely to think is fact. A different person, a different nuance to the lie. And they can cheat in a way a man deceiving another man cannot, unless, I suppose they are both gay. I will have to think about that one. But no man could lean forward and short-circuit my brain with his tits.

So, I find that Lucas Wainwright is writ large in cyberspace. Here, showing his holiday snaps being a daredevil; paragliding, surfing, well, posing with a surfboard, dressed in scuba gear. I wonder if he knows SCUBA stands for Self-Contained Underwater Breathing Apparatus? He looks like he would, and would bring it into every conversation. Do I dislike him because he looks like a smug git, or because Evie was terrorised by him? I'm not sure. Women use men. They have to. Right this minute I might be being used.

It takes only minutes, but I now know where he works, how long he has worked there, how he travels to work and where he lives. And that he likes a pint after work on a Friday night at a pub called the Dun Cow. Amazing what people will give away about themselves.

The next day I clean the Merc quickly and then head into the city, parking in a vastly expensive underground carpark in the centre of the city. I will use the trains from here. The firm Wainwright works for is called Dubbin, Lock and Symes. They seem to be some sort of building consultants. Lucas is in human resources. What do HR people actually do? I have never worked for a corporation and have only the faintest idea. Sack people legally is my take on it. Can't see any other reason for them. Anyway, the company is in a huge glass and steel tower block in Canary Wharf that looks prestigious.

I hang around and see him arrive. He is fairly tall, dark, exactly as Evie described and looks like his online pictures. He is wearing a three-piece dark suit with a dark lightweight coat billowing behind him. He moves as if reasonably fit. Sure enough he enters the building. No briefcase but a dark green backpack. I return to where I have left the Merc. I will need to clean it again before I go out to pick up Hohne.

That night Hohne calls me into his office. He is emptying documents out of his briefcase onto the desk. He flicks the 'on' switch on the computer but leaves it as I stand before his desk not quite at attention, but almost. He likes that. He sees himself as a general with troops. He isn't far wrong. He doesn't look up as he says,

'You went out this morning.'

'Yes sir.'

'Why?'

'I was curious about a man.'

Now he raises his eyes. 'And why is that?'

'I want to know if I like him or not.'

He stares at me for a long moment. I stare back. 'Is this man to do with my business?'

'No sir, personal.'

'Don't let it interfere with your duties.'

'No sir.'

As he pulls his keyboard towards him I turn to leave and bash my shin on a low table. As I bend to rub it, I peer under the screen and watch his fingers on the keypad. Muttering an apology, I leave.

Back in my room I write down what I think I saw. Hohne97?!. The question mark and exclamation mark may be wrong, but his hands went to the right middle of the keys then top left. Unimaginative. Perhaps he made his first million in 97? Or perhaps I followed his fingers incorrectly, but Hohne is no typist. He will have multiple passwords for his bank accounts, of course. I pause considering this. If I am right about his computer password, and if I am it is not by much, then he is a man who dislikes remembering long codes. My eyes fall on my own password notebook. It has shiny black covers and a spiral binder and is divided down the side into the alphabet. It is invaluable. Like everyone I have passwords for a dozen sites, some important, some not. I would think it a fairly certain bet that Hohne is the same. I wonder where he keeps it? I have decided to rob Hohne. The thought does not make me anxious.

The next day I meet Evie at the café we first saw each other at. She looks pleased to see me, but I can feel that I am uncertain. Exactly how much am I being used. We chat, and it isn't as comfortable as before. Fed up with dancing around what is worrying me, I lean across the table and ask, 'Why did you tell me his name?' I don't mean to sound aggressive, but I suspect I do. I watch her eyes to see if I can spot a lie. She colours up so easily, and I watch the heat rise up her face.

'You think I had an ulterior motive,' she says. All I can do is nod. She reaches across and lays one warm hand on mine. 'No, Marco, no. I wouldn't do that. Not to you nor to me. He threatened to kill any man I became involved with. I have no idea if what we have is 'involved' in his book or not. I haven't slept with you.' She hisses the last in a whisper.

'But he doesn't know where you live or work?'

'No, but I still work in London. I hope he is still out at Canary Wharf which is well away from my job here in the City, but it is still the same city. Still London. What if he finds me? What if he finds out about you? I couldn't bear it if he hurt you.'

'It is a city of over ten million people,' I point out.

'That is as may be, but I am still frightened.'

Is this why she hasn't slept with me? I feel pretty pissed off with this Lucas Wainwright. He has me courting a woman like a teenager when I want her underneath me and on top of a mattress. I give a grunt of frustration. Especially as Hohne wants me back by lunchtime on this precious Wednesday. Evie smiles at me,

'You are grunting your frustration, Beast.' She is smiling. I can't help it, I throw back my head and laugh. 'Ignore him, Marco. He is a horrid manipulative creep who I thought loved me. He doesn't know where I am and while it stays like that, you are safe.'

She lets me kiss her deeply before I leave her. She tastes of everything I want. We are tucked into a doorway with my body hiding her from the street. What am I doing? Kissing my woman in public? Because I can't have her to myself in private? Public displays of affection, it is called. PDAs. This is so not me. Lucas Wainwright has a great deal to answer for. I head back and my anger grows. It isn't just Evie this man is manipulating, but me.

Wainwright has told Evie that he will harm anyone she becomes involved with. That bothers me, why threaten the man? It is Evie he wishes to control. And what skills does he have? That statement suggests that he is willing to take on anyone of any shape or size. That makes no sense. I mean, he hasn't met me. I know I am far larger than he is, and used to violence. I got my first black eye at the age of five. In the dusty backstreets of an impoverished town, fighting was as normal as breathing. And as a trucker moving all around Europe I have run into my share of morons who needed teaching a lesson. I had once had to fight off an armed crew who thought they could just take my load and leave me in a ditch. I put four in the hospital and the fifth I tied up so the police could question him. But I have never started a fight; well, hardly ever and not as a proper grown up.

The Dunn Cow is walking distance from where Lucas lives, halfway between his tube stop from work and his front door. I amble in and order a pint. I am almost completely teetotal but here, looking around, I will need it for cover. Alcohol diminishes the reflexes and decision-making centres; I like to keep my control of myself sharp. There is a newspaper on the bar, rather creased and stained but I sweep it up as I make my way to a table at the back. Lucas is already there, hard against the wall, frowning at the outer door. I sit next to him, just a metre away, at the next table. The tables are small and round, but the back wall seating is a long dark-red plastic covered bench. He ignores me, I doubt he even registers my existence. I am dressed in a plain black tee shirt and non-descript black trousers. It should be jeans for what I hope he assumes I am, a tired worker-bee catching a beer before heading home. In one hand I have the pint glass, in the other the newspaper. It is the Sun, perfect cover for what I want and a stroke of luck. This paper does little serious news; a war breaking out perhaps, a factory fire, but mostly some unknown face two-timing a generic blonde. And is loved by builders and labourers everywhere. As cover it couldn't be better. I need him to underestimate me. And Sun readers are always, perhaps undeservedly, underestimated.

I am bent over the paper studying it as if I need to spell out the words one by one when I sense his attention sharpen. I lift my beer and my hand jolts, sending a small wave across the gold in the glass. Evie has just walked in. I am surprised at my reaction. My guts knot and I feel ice cold. I swallow, and stare at her wondering what she will say when she sees me here. Will she pretend she does not know me in front of Wainwright? Or the opposite. I stare, openly. Evie has her head down, shaking rain from a black umbrella. She must be wearing heels, high ones as she is taller. And then she sweeps damp hair from her face and I see her profile. Her nose is too sharp, her hair a little too long. It is an Evie clone, not my little Evie. I breathe in, steadying myself. It is not her. And that was when I decided that Evie had to be mine. As I was hers.

I head back to the car keeping my head on the turn. The rain inter-feres with my hearing so I need to be even more alert than usual. I reach the car without incident, not that I expected one and open the boot. I remove a huge towel and place it over the leather seat before I climb in. I will have to be up very early tomorrow to have the Merc ready for Hohne, but it was worth it. All the way home my mind sings, she told the truth, she told the truth. I also wonder if I should be disgusted with myself for doubting her. But, no, I have picked up more from Hohne than I realise. Trust no one, check everything, then check again. It isn't a comfortable thought. But it is now who I am.

I sleep well that night, deep and long. I will have Evie. One day. And I can be patient. I don't want to be, but I will be. For her.

Saturday is the regular run to Felixstowe and the tour of Hohne's 'business' haunts all night. On Sunday I am unexpectedly back early. I had taken Hohne to a hotel, Claridges, in Mayfair. He meets a woman there and this is another regular run and I wait to drive him home, but when he climbs into the car he snaps at me that I can have the rest of the night off. It is only six, so a gift. He is in a furious temper. In the past he has always smelt freshly showered and of new cologne when he re-entered the car. Post sex clean-up, I always assumed. From now on it seems I have Sundays free. They are of no use to me as Evie is visiting her mother. From his fury, I assume it is the woman who dumped Hohne and not the other way around. The idea cheers me.

It is two in the morning later in the week and I am considering going to bed. I have been watching DVDs. Evie sent me a 'Good night' text at eleven, and I check my phone just to confirm that she has not sent anything else I have missed. Foolish, I know. I am about to tug off my tee shirt when the phone rings. It has to be Evie. I snatch it up and hear her panting, then a scream before,

'Get away from me! Get away! Why are you here, why? What do you want with me?' and then the phone is dropped to the floor and I can hear a man's voice. I need no more. I am out of the house and shooting out of the gates in Hohne's Merc in seconds. I leave my door open and my gun in the drawer, but I have my knife on my calf. Like I told Evie, it only comes off when I am asleep. I reach my first red light, edge forward glancing both ways, then floor the car, at the next one I am across even faster. London is not asleep, but equally, it isn't heaving.

I reach Evie's in minutes that feel like hours. The front door to the block is swinging open, so someone has broken the lock. I tear through and take the steps two and three at a time, but when I reach her door I slow, and take two deep breaths. I edge forward carefully and nudge against the door. It swings open gently. I step forward and peer in. Evie is holding what might be a bread board in front of her as a shield but her fingers are exposed. Not good. She should be using the wooden board as a weapon.

I edge into the room as quietly as possible, but Evie spots me and cannot hide her expression of relief. There is a man between her and me wearing a black tracksuit with the hood up. It might be Wainwright, but it could be anyone. He doesn't turn, which surprises me. Most attackers or thieves, if they are aware someone is behind them immediately turn, but this man doesn't. I should have paid more attention to this, and the second mistake I make is assuming that I am entering a fist fight.

Surprise gone, I kick a coffee table out of the way and step forward, my arm out ready to grab him by the back of the neck. But he leaps forward, away from me and towards Evie. She gives another scream, and shoves the bread board up to cover her face, but the man is determined to reach her. I step forward again, fast, and kick out his knee. That should disable him enough to make him think of something else other than Evie. Instead, he swings around and a massive knife cuts into my shoulder. Shocked, I step back, but now he is on me. It is Wainwright, and he looks utterly crazed. I shove up my left arm to grasp his right, but he tosses the knife to his left and stabs forward towards my gut. Again, I feel the shock of impact, but little pain. I think he has missed, until warmth begins to leak down to my waist. Hell, I have two injuries and he isn't stopping.

'Ring the police!' I yell at Evie as I step back and trip on the coffee table. The trip saves my face as the knife once more slashes in my direction. This time I know what I am up against and I go for him with everything I have. I leap forward and body barge him and we fall to the floor in a welter of arms, legs, and the knife. I have to get the knife. I am bleeding from at least three wounds now, he has also caught me on my upper left arm. I am not too sure what happens next. I raise my fist and punch into his face, I know I do that, but then I remember it later only as a blur. We struggle and fight some more, but for how long I have no idea. When I finally stand I have the knife in my hand and he is lying still. What have I done? I am panting and sweating as I hear sirens, and blue lights now swirl on the ceiling. Evie rushes to me and instead of hugging me, she kneels at my feet and hauls up my trouser leg. I can see that her hands are shaking as she unbuckles the straps, but I don't understand what she is doing, my brain does not seem to be able to make sense of what I am seeing. She rushes to the kitchen window, yanks it open, and my knife complete with sheath goes sailing out into the night. I have no idea what is at the back of her block, nor where the knife may go. She runs back and checks my trouser legs just as the first police arrive. There are shouts of 'Police, police,' and Evie staggers to the door. She pulls the door open and falls into the arms of the first officer, who seems unsurprised and hauls her backwards, out of the room. The second officer steps in and regards me. She has her taser out and it is pointing towards me.

'Drop the knife!' she yells.

I look at it and frown, then let it go. I stare down at it for a moment, and there is a strange silence in the room with no one moving. 'I think I have killed a man,' I say, and collapse down on the sofa with my head in my bloody hands.

'Are you wounded?' she demands. I am not sure what to say, everything seems unreal. Then I hear Evie shouting, she sounds desperate, 'He is wounded,' she is yelling, 'he needs help.' I look up at the police officer who is putting her taser away. 'Let's have a look at you, sir.'

I want to laugh. One minute I am being threatened with a taser, and the next this woman is impersonally checking to see if my injuries are life threatening. 'Paramedics are on their way,' she says, matter-of-factly. I love the UK police. Anywhere else and I reckon I would be having the stuffing kicked out of me simply for existing and spoiling their night. Or shot. That is always a possibility in some countries.

Evie disappears and I begin to stand, 'Where are you taking her?' I ask, 'She hasn't done anything.' I am frantic and the officer puts a firm hand on my shoulder and presses me down again. 'It's alright, sir, she is being taken to hospital. Her injuries aren't serious, but I am not so sure about yours and I'd like the medics to look at you before we move you.'

I am still dazed as my jacket is eased off me, my tee shirt is cut away, and

I am bandaged. The initial shoulder wound is shallow, and the gut one is also fairly minor, but the slash into my left arm was meant to do some damage. 'Could have been worse,' the medic says cheerfully. I scowl at him. I worked to build that muscle and now it is severed in half. 'Don't know,' the officer says standing back and looking at me, 'nearly lost his meat and potatoes with that one.' She is pointing to my stomach wound that slashes at an angle stopped only by my belt buckle. I have no idea what she means.

When I am patched up the medic says, 'How do you feel? On a scale of one to ten, how much pain are you in?'

'Not much,' I say.

The medic turns to the police lady, 'Shock and adrenaline. He needs to go to hospital, that arm wound needs stitching.'

'Ok,' she says, I will come in the ambulance with you.

I am laid on a trolley and I want to protest, but my head is spinning. I have been wounded before. This is not too bad, not worthy of being carried, but it is clear I have no say in the matter. The ambulance feels too bright and I close my eyes, but the medic keeps shaking me and talking to me. I wish he would piss off.

I am stitched back together in Accident and Emergency. The woman in the next bay, separated from me and my police lady by nothing more than a thin curtain is being told off. Politely. It seems she dropped an ironing board on her foot. The doctor or nurse is explaining to her that a bruised foot does not constitute sufficient reason to go to A and E in the middle of the night. 'But I have been here since four this afternoon,' she says indignantly, 'and I may have a broken bone.' 'You shouldn't be here at all,' an exhausted voice says.

'Hey lady,' I call, 'I have three knife wounds. I should be here, so why don't you go home.'

The police lady looks shocked and hisses, 'You are not helping. Be quiet.' I shrug. No one where I come from would go to the hospital with such a minor injury. When I am bandaged up the police lady says,

'Do you feel well enough to come to the station and be interviewed?'

I nod, then say, 'I'd like to get it over with. But,' I look up at her, 'I can't remember all of it. Some of it is a blur.'

'Well, tell us what you can,' she says calmly, and her easy manner relaxes me. I may have committed murder, but there is nothing I can do about it now.

At the station I am stripped, including my shoes and socks, and given a pair of paper pants and a white all-in-one. I have seen them on tv, but never in real life. They are uncomfortable against bare skin. I am breathalysed, given drug tests, then sat down in a small windowless room with a cup of tea. I ask for the painkillers that the policewoman was given to hold for me; I am beginning to throb.

Two men walk in and begin the interview. They are calm and matter of fact. I am beginning to shake a little. I have taken a life. What have I become? I am cautioned and formally arrested. I tell them of Evie's panicked phone call, of my dash across town, of the Merc slung against yellow lines. They take the registration number and call for someone to stick a Police Aware notice on it. I think the keys are still in it and they offer to lock it up and bring the them back. I tell them who I think the man is, and that the knife is his. We go through the time-line a few times from when I step into the room until when my mind is blank. I hear myself repeating, 'I killed a man,' but the relevant part of my mind does not seem to be able to explain to either them or me how that happened. I am becoming exhausted and start to slump onto the table. They tell me they will speak to me again, but as far as they are concerned, I am free to go, although I may be re-arrested later for murder. I am not to leave the country. For the first time I find something about the night humorous, 'Chance would be a fine thing,' I mutter.

As I begin to rise from my chair two other men enter. One is tall and thin, almost bald, wearing a shabby suit that looks as if he has slept in it, the other is plump and a far sharper dresser. His tie looks silk and I immediately wonder if he is on the take; perhaps he belongs to Hohne. And then I realise that I would not have known it was silk but for my time with Hohne. That man has influenced me more than I like. Here I am, me, judging suit quality. Nausea roils.

The two men introduce themselves and once more turn on the tape recorder. I don't take in their names, I am too tired. We go through what I now recognise as the usual preliminaries and then they ask,

'You work for a Mr Hohne.'

'Yes.' How do they know that already? It wasn't a question.

'Why does he employ you?'

'I drive him and attend meetings with him.'

'You attend meetings?'

'Yes.'

'What do you do at these meetings?'

'I stand and look large.'

'You don't take part in what is being discussed.'

I give a cough of a laugh. 'No.'

'So you are security. Why does he need security?'

'He says he sometimes has bearer bonds either in the car or in his briefcase. He has explained that these bonds are like money, notes, but are untraceable. If anyone took them from him, he could not get the money back. I am there to suggest that robbing him is not a good idea.'

'Has anyone ever tried to rob him?'

'Not while I have been working for him.'

'You must be very effective.' Now it is the tall detective who is speaking.

'I suppose so.'

'Are you armed when you are working?'

'Not with a weapon. I have had martial arts training and weight lift and so on, but I have not been in a fight before tonight of any kind since I was a boy in Serbia.'

'Really?' Disbelief pours across the table and I smile.

'It is the truth.' I shrug. Either they believe me or they don't. I am not a man men pick fights with. The occasional scrap when I was on the road I ignore. They were not fights; not like tonight.

'How long have you worked for him?'

'Three years, look, what is this? I was in a fight tonight. I am told the man died? Why are you not asking me about that? My employer was not there and the argument had nothing to do with him.'

'You are a very interesting man, Mr Ilîc.'

'No.' I shake my head, this time the disbelief is all mine. 'I am the most boring man you could meet. I live above a garage, I drive a car, I work out. My life is exactly what you see, dull.'

'Perhaps that is what puzzles us, Mr Ilîc. No one is ever that dull.'

'I promise you, I am.'

'Until you met Mrs Wainwright.'

'I do not know that name. I met Eve Scott in a café.'

'But the man you killed was Mr Wainwright.'

'So I understand. All I knew was that Evie rang me in a panic. I went to her apartment and found a man there with a large knife in her face. He was shouting at her and she had a board up to shield her face. You have seen the bruising, he had already hurt her.'

'Yes. So what did you do?'

'I have already told the others.'

'Tell us again, now we want to hear it.'

'I lifted my boot and kicked out his knee. I expected him to fall to the floor where I could then take the knife from him. I was shouting at Evie to call the police.'

'She had already called us.'

'I know that now. I did not know then.'

'What happened?'

I shake my head. That is a very good question. 'I am not sure. Instead of going down he spun around and slashed my shoulder open.'

'Then what did you do?'

I look into the detective's eyes. 'It hurt. I hit him.' I have a thick white bandage around my left shoulder, a large patch on my gut and my left bicep is bound up and going a bit pink as the blood seeps through. Oh, and a black eye. What does he think I did? I fought for my life.

'Should I have let him cut me again? Hurt Evie?'

'Ah, Mrs Wainwright.'

'Eve Scott,' I interrupt. 'She told me that she changed her name with a lawyer.'

'Ah, did she? So you knew it was not her real name?'

'What is a real name? It was her legal name and the only one I knew.'

'Are you lovers?'

'Wha ... ? No, no we are not. I like her. She was sitting in a café trying not to cry. I wanted to make her feel better. We talked. Became friends. Coffee friends.'

'Coffee friends.'

I don't respond. I am very tired and I am sick of this. 'Mr Policeman, are you going to arrest me? I admit what I did. That the man died, I am very sorry, but I am not sorry for fighting him. He hurt me and wanted to hurt Evie and he was waving a huge knife around intending to harm someone. It could have been you if you had arrived earlier.' I now know that Evie called the police before calling me. I suspect she only called me because no comforting blue lights appeared. She should not have needed me and he knows it.

'We are not arresting you for murder at present. Clearly there will be an investigation and you are not to leave the country. Meanwhile, what is Mr Hohne's business?'

'Why are you asking about him again?'

'He is a person of interest to us.'

'What I see is of no interest. He lives in a big house. Six days a week he goes to different places to conduct business. Sometimes he travels. He does a lot of talking. On Sundays he goes out for the day and I often do not know where. His life is almost as dull as mine.'

'But what is the business?'

I shrug. How should I know?

'You must have some idea.'

'Finance of some kind?' It is a question. I may suspect, but I know very little. And what I know I do not intend to share.

'Saturday you took him to Felixstowe port.'

'Yes.'

'Do you go there often?'

'Yes. He has a small office at the docks.'

'Does he have other offices?'

'A smart one in London. It is in 22 Bishopsgate.'

'Very expensive.'

'As is his car and his house. He seems to be rich and he pays my wages.'

'Is it a good wage?'

'Much better than I can earn as a lorry driver.'

'Ah yes, that is how you came to this country, did you not.' The tall one again.

I am not completely sure I understand his meaning, so I say nothing. Then I frown, 'I am here legally. I have all my papers.'

'Oh yes. We already know that.' He is so bland it is threatening. The police in every country can do as they will. This man could lock me up for life, I think, and it sends a shiver down my spine. I have great admiration for the police in this country, but that doesn't mean that right now I am not afraid of them.

'How much trouble am I in?' I ask.

'Mr Hohne,' the tall one says again.

I scrub my face with my hands. 'What time is it please? You have taken my watch and my phone.'

'Eight thirty.'

'Has anyone told Mr Hohne where I am? He will be expecting me to be at work.'

The tall one spins a phone across the table towards me. 'Ring him.'

I stare at the phone as if it is poisoned. 'Ring him?' I did not expect this.

'Go ahead. We wouldn't want to get you into trouble.'

So I do as instructed. Hohne picks up after four rings. I have already put the phone on loudspeaker and sat it on the table in front of me. Hohne's deep voice fills the room, 'Who is this?'

'It is Marco Ilîc, Mr Hohne, I am in a police station.'

'And why is that?'

'A man attacked me with a knife. He has injured me and I fought back and the police tell me he has died from his injuries.'

'Have you been cautioned or arrested.'

'No sir.'

'Then leave. I need you here.'

'On my way sir.'

Before I can end the call he says, 'Oh, and Marco, if they don't allow you to leave ring me back. I will send my lawyer.'

I breathe a sigh of relief that all the parties hear. 'Thank you sir. I am grateful.'

I close down the phone and spin it across the table to the older detective. I stand and say, 'I am going home.'

'Not to your real home,' the tall one says. I don't bother to answer.

'Do I have to travel home in this?' I gesture down my body. The two detectives exchange a glance.

'We have a locker with clothes. You should be able to find something to wear, ask the custody sergeant.'

The clothes will smell of other men's sweat and fear, but I am in no position to argue. My tee shirt was cut to shreds and the police took my trousers and shoes to analyse for blood splatters.

'Don't leave the country,' one of the detectives instructs me.

I turn to look at him. 'What, not even to Serbia?' I try to keep my voice even, but he can hear the sneer I was trying to cover. I have not slept, and I need to cross London to return to Hohne, get clean and dressed, and then drive Hohne into number 22. Traffic will be shit and I have had no sleep. And where on earth is the Merc?

By the time I have some clothes and have been allowed to head down the steps outside the police station, the commuter traffic is already intense. It is not going to be a good day and I have a headache.

It is nine before I walk once more up the drive to Hohne's house. I report immediately to his office as I know that is what he will want me to do without him having to spell it out.

'What happened?' His voice is a bark.

'I met a lady in a café. We talked, made friends just a little. Conversation friends.'

'Conversation friends?' His voice is mocking but I am trying to impress upon him that we are not lovers. If he thinks we are, he might turn on Evie.

'Only that. She rang last night in a panic. She is divorced, but her ex-husband had turned up at her flat. She had called the police but they had not shown. He had a huge knife, almost a machete.' At that Hohne's eyebrows raised. 'Worse, I took the Merc and I think it is still parked on double yellow lines outside her apartment.'

'I sent DePaul for it some time ago. It is in the garage. I will use the Jaguar for a while. I am bored with the Mercedes. Take some time off. Sleep. See a doctor if you need to. As soon as you are fit I want you back at work.'

I force myself out and across to my apartment. I stand looking up the stairs that lead to my door and sigh. I drag myself up by hanging onto the handrail. Once inside, I strip and put all of the second-hand clothes and the disgusting blue and white sliders they gave me for my feet, in a bin bag and tie it tight. I go and run a basin with warm water and do what my mother did before my brother and I installed a decent bathroom in their house, I strip wash with a flannel and soap. As all my injuries are on my upper body I can wipe around the bandages and then swing my legs up into the basin and wash my feet, one after another. Just like Mama used to do. The memory is warm. Then I collapse into bed and pass out with exhaustion.

I wake with a start as the fire door opens. I know who it is by her outline against the evening sky. I have slept all day. I swing my legs out of bed and go over and pull her gently into my arms.

'You shouldn't be here,' I say, as my hands search through her hair, around her shoulders and down her arms, press against the flat areas of her back. I can't stop searching for broken bones, or painful bruising. Being able to touch her soothes my heart.

'Marco, I am alright, I promise. They let me out of hospital an hour ago.'

'Why were you there so long?'

'A brain scan, it took a while and it is not important.'

How can she say that? 'If they did it, then it is important. What was the result?'

'They will tell me tomorrow. I will get a message on my phone. Now stop worrying, and let me examine you.'

'I am fine,' I insist, 'and you really shouldn't be here. I saw it on tv once, you could be charged with, oh, what is the word, it begins with a C?'

'Collusion,' she says, and I nod, which hurts. Then she hands me my knife. 'I went to find this first. I didn't want the police to find it with both of our fingerprints on it.'

I am astonished. She is good at thinking, little Evie. I go to put my arm around her but she shakes me off.

'Come back to bed,' she insists.

'Oh, princess, exactly the words I once longed to hear from you, but not now. I might be charged with murder, and I don't want you involved any more than you are.'

I am shoved firmly in the chest, which jars my stomach wound. 'Get back to bed, I need to sleep, and I want you next to me.' I give in. I am still too worn out to argue. How is it in those hero films the guy always gets up with bullet wounds and saves the world? All I want to do is curl up and sleep. She returns to lock the outer door, then strips down to a tee shirt and panties and crawls into my bed. I slide in beside her, and we hold each other until sleep hits us.

We wake in the early hours. 'I need a shower,' is whispered in my ear, and then she is gone. I lay and stare at the ceiling and wonder if she will come back. When she does, her hair is wet and she smells of my soap. I like it. She places a coffee beside me and then slides back into bed. We sit, sipping and staring in parallel. We have matching black eyes and it makes me want to grin. 'How did he find you?' I ask. Translated, it means, did you tell him? Because you had met me?

She breathes in deep. 'The police have been investigating. Now he is dead, his juvenile record can be examined whereas before it was sealed. At fourteen he was given a warning about peering into a girl's window, and at fifteen, accused of keeping a girl in his room without letting her go home. He had gagged and tied her up but said it was a joke. At seventeen, he was charged with rape but the case was dropped due to lack of evidence. Then it goes quiet until the night he attacked me. Because of that, the police have been trawling CCTV evidence, and have found him hanging around outside where I work and then following me home. He had maps all over his home study. He had been methodically searching for me. They are curious about the quiet period, and what he was up to. I told them that he had me, his living breathing blow-up doll.' Her voice is bitter.

'Hey, you kiss a lot of frogs before you find a prince.' I heard a girl on the Tube say that once. At least it makes Evie laugh.

'He was worse than a frog. He was a skunk.'

I have other words for him, but I will keep them to myself. We get up to eat toast and eggs and drink more coffee. 'Let's hire a car and go to the coast,' Evie suggests. So we do. Evie drives and I doze as the sun beats in through the windscreen.

The sun is shining in Brighton. We pay a king's ransom for parking, eat fish and chips and then an ice cream, all of which is seriously good, and walk on a pebbly beach. And we hold hands. And chat. About nothing and little. It is a good day, and I wrap it up in my memory to keep forever.

Evie once more insists on driving us back and we return the car to the hire place. As we leave the office she takes my hand and we walk back to her apartment. The outer door is off its hinges and propped against the wall. I feel Evie shudder so firm my grip on her hand. Blue and white police tape spider-webs her front door, but Evie ignores it and climbs through. We stand together in the centre of the room and gaze around. The coffee table I remember breaking, but the tv is smashed, the sofa has huge knife slashes in it, and there is smashed crockery all over the floor. I can read his travel through the place. Kitchen to create fear, sofa to create terror, then Evie herself, trapped against the far wall with her pitiful shield. Rage grows. Pointless, as he is gone now and cannot threaten her again. Evie returns to my side with a back pack. 'Can we go to your place?' she asks, and I nod. I am feeling much stronger, but not strong enough to send her away.

We buy take-away food and call an Uber to Hohne's place. At mine, we eat and chat, and then Evie insists that I shower and she re-do my bandages. I scratch my chin and stare at her. Her eyes, as she looks back at me are both amused and determined. I give in. Whatever Evie wants of me, she can have, and she knows it. I think the expression is 'Pussy whipped', which is funny considering our relationship so far. I go into my bathroom and strip. No one leaves years in any army with physical modesty. Knowing she is standing close behind me makes me as hard as a rock. I gaze down at the very physical evidence that I am feeling more than well and am close to the woman I want and shrug. I can't hide it; it is what it is.

'You have a gorgeous backside,' she says, and I snort with laughter, and step into the shower. As I turn to face her, a naked Evie steps in beside me. I don't have much to thank Hohne for, but a decent sized bathroom is one thing. She slides a soapy hand down my chest, skirts my gut wound, and then soaps the very protuberant sign of my lust. As I throw my head back and groan, she has the widest smile on her face, she is a witch.

'Oh, Marco, I knew you wouldn't disappoint.'

'Been dreaming of me, have you?' I ask. Hell, I am a finger's width away from shooting my load right now. I pull her to me kiss her with the water pounding down on our heads and her blissfully soapy skin sliding against mine. I finally let her go to say, 'I want you right now, Princess.'

Her grin says it all, but the topping on the cake is when she whispers, 'Good!' in my ear. I go to pick her up, but she slides away from me and steps out of the shower.

'First,' she demands, 'I am going to re-do your bandages.'

I can't disagree, making love with soggy and grubby padding spotted all over me is not my idea of fun either. Besides, I too want to see how everything is healing. My guts are now green and purple from the kicking Wainwright gave me, but the gut wound is closed already. He had only sliced open the skin, and I am guessing that it looked so much worse because it took so long to get me patched up there was time for the blood stain to become impressive. The cut on my shoulder is similarly shallow. It is my left bicep that is the problem one. It went fairly deep. I flex my arm and there is no fresh bleeding, so I allow Evie to patch me over. As she places each piece of white muslin she kisses the area. While she does that I slide my hands over her backside and anywhere else I can reach that won't distract her too much.

'Marco,' she chides. But my grin is huge and she kisses me on the nose. That doesn't stop me. Her skin is like rose petals and slides under my rough hands like a completely different substance to my calloused palms. She has lain a towel over my lap and it tents nicely. I see her glance down a couple of times, and my grin becomes so wide it hurts. I wonder if she is the kind of woman to go down on a man, and that doesn't lessen the tenting any.

Getting to the bed is easy, when I am fed up with being nursed, I stand and catch her up into my arms. 'Don't you dare undo my good work,' she orders, but she is laughing. She weighs nothing. I life heavier weights than this daily, but I don't lower them with the care I use as I settle her down onto the sheets. I slide in beside her, then roll on top. She opens her legs to cradle me and I give a sigh of pure contentment. Keeping my weight on my arms I lean over and kiss her. Her flavour is addictive. For the first time I sweep the inside of her mouth with my tongue, and feel her pull away from me.

'What is wrong?'

'I ...'

'Don't tell me no one ever tongued you before?'

'Not like that.' Her voice is a whisper.

'But you were married?' I feel her shrug.

'I didn't like his kisses, so we didn't much.'

I take my weight onto one arm and stroke her hair from her face. There is much I need to learn about her so-called marriage. 'Did you dislike everything with him?'

Her already pink cheeks turn fire-engine red. 'Yes.' The word is barely audible.

'Good, because I like tasting you. In fact, I like every tiny bit of you. I may even nibble your toes.'

Her eyes open wide and she giggles. 'Don't you dare!'

'Ok. We will leave that to one side.' Then I kiss her again, letting my tongue adore the taste of her. When she feels limp, and her hands are stroking my back, I kiss her neck. The so-soft skin under her chin, the small area under her ear. I nuzzle and soothe and she sinks back into the mattress, boneless. So I begin to enjoy myself. I nibble and kiss my way down her body, rubbing my face into her rounded belly, loving the softness of her, so different from my hard-won muscles. Where I am mahogany, she is cashmere.

I suspect she will pull away if I go too low, so I kiss down the outside of her thigh, worshiping her with my mouth. At her knee, I turn inwards, nibbling up the inside of her thigh. As expected, she pulls away a little, once more aware of where she is.

'Marco?'

'Hush, little one. Let me worship you. Say 'stop', and I will. I always will. Wherever we are, whatever we are doing.'

'Perhaps I should be doing some worshiping of my own?' Her voice is deeper, breathy, and I smile, pressing my face into her glorious body.

I huff into her curls some more until I am sure she has forgotten where she is or what she is doing but is simply feeling. I am desperate to plunge into her, but want so much to give her pleasure. She may not come for me, I know. Many women die never knowing or under-standing what their own bodies are capable of. Perhaps their bodies cannot, though, me? I think it is the mind that prevents the roil of plea-sure. I rock my hips into the mattress to soothe myself, I am hard as iron, so hard I fear I may fracture into pieces. But I concentrate as I begin to taste and lick, suck and soothe, nip and kiss. Her back arches and I hold her backside firm, loving its rich softness. Then I take a risk, and slide one finger inside. She is the very definition of bliss; soft, moist, and mine. Her muscles contract, so tight, I am close to losing myself into the sheets. I push in two, and thrust and withdraw, crooking my fingers slightly. She explodes, her body convulsing and I hold her safe. As her voice softens to a murmur I think that it is a good thing that the Bentley below us does not have ears. I slide up her body to hold her safe.

'Marco?' she whispers.

My voice is gravel. 'I want you.'

'Then have me,' and she grins, an expression of pure happiness that I put there.

I have never felt like this before. The only word my mind can find is 'worshipful'. I am not even sure it is a proper word. I edge into her a little and hold still. She is so hot, she boils me. Then I nudge deeper. She is tight. I wonder why, but stop wondering as sensation takes me. I ease back, then move deep, keeping to a steady pace as I feel her begin to relax once more beneath me.

'Are you alright?' I whisper.

'Never better,' is the response. She is clutching my upper arms, letting her hands ride the bulge and relax of my biceps as I rock in and out. I am close already. Holding, lasting, is a sign of control, the same as lifting a weight that is just a little too heavy. Concentration and muscle control are essential. I pride myself on my weight lifting. I used to pride myself on this, but the feel of her is racing me to explosion. I want her too much, far too much. I can't help myself, too soon I can feel that I am lost, soaring into pleasure. I flick a thumbpad over her between her curls and her eyes fly open in shock. Her cheeks glow with arousal. It is a beautiful sight to me. As I pump my last, seismic pleasure rocks me. Already I know I want her to be my last. My only. But fate is unlikely to grant me that. I hold her in my arms as another orgasm bucks her body and she arches. I will hold her safe until it is over and she is herself again.

She slides down into the mattress, satiated and content. I feel rather smug. I curl her into me and wrap around her. 'Sleep,' I whisper, and she does. I let myself slide into a doze, and recognise that in that moment, I am exactly where I long to be.

Chapter Seven

I awake to the smell of coffee. It seems my princess has mastered my coffee machine. I shove myself upright and rip the dressing off my gut and shoulder wounds. Already they are sealed and knitted together. My guts are now mostly green and yellow with only some purple, so all is good there. My bicep injury, the only one that really annoys me, is still painful, but at a level that is easily bearable.

Evie has pulled on one of my tee shirts. 'I have worn that,' I tell her. 'It should go into the wash basket.'

'No, it smells of you and I like that,' and she climbs in beside me. Okay then, I think.

'Marco, we need to talk.' Ah, the tee shirt thing I liked, this not so much.

'About?'

'Lots of things. First, did you think that I became your friend because I hoped you would deal with Lucas for me?'

Whew. I let out a gusty breath and wonder just how much truth is good for a couple? All I can think is that if I lose her for telling the truth, it is better than losing her later because I am caught out in a lie. I suspect my hesitation has answered for me in any case.

'I did wonder.'

'It was the opposite. I kept you at arms-length because I didn't want Lucas to ever find out about you, and I don't know, secrets seem impossible to keep. You are so beautiful, and so strong, he would never have taken you on face-to-face, but a knife in the back on a quiet street from a man you have never met would be something even you might not be able to defeat.'

'So did you always want to sleep with me?' Ok, so it is a dumb question, but I am male and it is the only one I want answered.

She puts her mug of coffee down and reaches round to kiss me. And swirls her coffee-tongue around mine. I growl in my throat, and she giggles through the kiss. 'Always,' she whispers into my mouth. As she pulls away, I narrow my eyes at her. 'Later,' she says, in her bossy voice. 'Also, I know Hohne. I have been out to dinner with him twice. Did you really believe that any sensible woman would come in through that back gate and climb to your place on her own? I knew as soon as you mentioned him that if any of his minions found me and strong-armed me to him, he would be unlikely to harm me.'

All thoughts of more sex whisk out of my mind. 'What?'

'Marco, what do you think I do for a living?'

As my mind is blasted into pieces presently, I struggle to come up with an answer. 'Office work?' I offer.

'Mm, and I would bet that you think all office work is the same, just foolish indoor people shuffling unimportant pieces of paper.' Well, that sums it up pretty accurately. I mean, what else can it involve? 'And you have never asked me what I did at university.' To be absloutely honest, I am not completely sure what a university is or does. I give a nod, and hope that is enough. 'Well, I did computer sciences and business studies. And it bored me. So I stopped going to lectures and just read and researched what I wanted to do. At the end of the first year I had to go to see my tutor who said I was being thrown out as I hadn't attended any lectures. I told him that they weren't worth going to, and showed him my notes. After four years they awarded me a PhD. I believe I am only the second woman to ever be awarded a doctorate without doing a first degree; Jane Goodall was the first. But I was all work and no play, so when Lucas showed interest in me, I was overwhelmed and fell into his hand like an overripe fruit.'

'Hey,' I say, and hug her, 'don't be so hard on yourself. He was a predator from the sound of it. What defences would any woman have against a man like him?'

'I was such a fool. We married within six months. I had been snapped up by a big US bank, and was earning a fortune. To be honest, I didn't know what to do with all that money. So I worked, and came home to Lucas who told me I was wonderful and then asked for his dinner. After I left Lucas I joined the bank I now work for. They offered me even more money and a junior partnership.'

'So what do you do?'

'I manage the personal finances for individuals. At first, I was excited. My research had been on financial flow, and here I could put it into practice. My job is to manage people's investments so that they maximise their profits. I attempt to predict trends, which is almost impossible, but my algorithms are right at least 65% of the time. The problem with the stock market is it is basically gambling. You put money on a stock and gamble that it will go up. When people want stock, the price does go up. If they stop wanting it, it goes down. And the reasons for the up and down are often opinion and have nothing to do with the value of the company. Are you still with me?'

Was I? I gave a nod. Frankly, my eyeballs were spinning.

'My work takes a lot of the guesswork out of which stock to keep and which to lose. I am making our customers a great deal of money. A truism of money is that the more you have the more you make. Rich people find it easy to get richer.' And poor people like my Mama and Tata stay poor, I think. But Evie hasn't finished. 'The problem is, I was sitting alone in my apartment after I left Lucas afraid to go out. He wasn't at all happy about me going, and at the time I was terrified of him. I lived as if I was permanently walking on eggs, frightened of his disapproval. It is hard to explain. Anyway, all that new spare time was boring, so I began to research our customers. All I wanted to do was know them better so I could do a better job for them. But the more I researched the more I realised that everyone I looked at was Russian mafia or something equally as horrible. I began to be afraid for a different reason, and then I decided not to be afraid. A lot of these men are stupid, and I am not.'

She is looking at me as if I am supposed to understand what she is saying. All I want to know is how well she knows Hohne or, more to the point, what Hohne knows about her.

'Hohne is one of the most stupid.' Now I really prick up my ears. 'Like many self-made men, Hohne doesn't trust anyone. Especially women. I have advised him where and how to put his money, but for most of it, he prefers to do it all himself. Believe me, that is utterly stupid. As a result, I have access to most of his bank accounts. With a couple of his passwords, I could empty the lot tomorrow.'

My eyes nearly pop out of my head. Clearly, Evie knows stuff I can only imagine. She is sitting there, looking smug, and I am utterly stunned. 'You could?' I say, and my voice is husky with incredulity. All she does is widen her smile and nod. Then she adds, 'I can take the money, but how do I get away with it? I can hide from the authorities that it was me, but not from Hohne. He would know straight away.'

It is a puzzle. 'So why were you having dinner with him?' I can feel how my hackles have risen.

'The first time was a general dinner of the bank's board and a few invitees. I had met him in the office a number of times when I was introduced to him as being his personal banker, and I could feel him watching me across the room. Initially it made me uneasy as he reminded me of Lucas, of the way he used to watch me. The second time I was tricked. I thought it was another general dinner, but there were only four of us, two senior board members, Hohne, and myself. The two board members ate, then stood, made some limp excuses, and left. At which point Hohne put his hand on my knee. As I lifted it off he said something like, 'When you are ready, I will be waiting.' I had no idea what he meant, but he seemed so sure of himself, and that was scary. By that point all my loyalty to the bank had vanished; they had set me up, practically handed me over to Hohne. I was determined as I walked out of there to find another job. To be honest, I have been so obsessed with you, I haven't got around to it.'

'Really?' That is all the encouragement I need. Within seconds I have tugged Evie down under the sheets and my hands and tongue are busy. Who needs money when they have a warm and willing woman. I lift my head for a moment from where I am suckling at her breast, apparently from the way she is writhing with her full consent, and ask,

'What's he worth?'

'About 9.5 billion pounds.'

'Ok,' I say, and go back to what I am doing. My mind goes, he can't be that stupid then, can he? And then I forget to think.

Afterwards we go out to eat, and make plans. Evie has a list. 'We need fake passports, a plastic surgeon and a decision on where to live.'

'A plastic surgeon?' I ask, my eyes bugging out.

'You my beautiful beast need that bump in your nose smoothing out and your jaw making a little less angular. The surgeon will be the best one to advise us.'

I blink, and stroke my chin. 'I like my face,' I say, 'I have lived with it for a long time.'

'Facial recognition,' she says emphatically. 'We both need enough so that we look sufficiently different not to be picked up by cameras. It doesn't have to be much, just a shaving of bone here and there.' I do not like the sound of this. 'And your arm tattoo, that needs lasering off. It is a bit blurred anyway, so you can have a crisp new one done on top.' My tattoo is a remnant of my army days. But I have to admit, it wasn't well done in the first place, and not only does it say army, it says Serb army, and we weren't everyone's chocolate biscuit. Evie has clearly given this a lot of thought. I am not sure what kind of daydream this is, but it is beyond surreal.

'Then,' she says, 'we need to ensure Hohne is arrested and put away for a long time.'

No, I think, for anyone to get away with this, we need him dead. But that I don't say. My army nightmares drove me to hauling trucks all over Europe for years; feeling the knife slide into Wainwright will keep me awake for another ten. I am not sure even billions of pounds are worth the guilt of taking yet another life. Even his.

'How much can you give the police?' she asks. Now that is a question. 'A lot, and nothing,' I say, and wonder exactly how much I do know, and if any of it is any use. And if I would risk my life giving it to anyone. Or Evie's.

'Who do you have left that you care about? You have an elder brother in Germany you have lost touch with, and your mother and father. Is there anyone else who Hohne could use to threaten you with?'

I look her straight in the eye. 'You,' I say.

'Don't worry about me. Now I have survived Lucas I am not afraid of anything anymore.'

I breathe in deep. The woman is a fool. But, for now, she is my fool. She is pressing on, 'Where would your parents be willing to move to? How about Canada? There is a lot of country to get lost in in Canada.'

I shake my head. 'Don't you think I would have moved them years ago? Hohne knows as well as me that the streets they live in are their whole world. They were born, courted, married, bore their children and will die with the same people who they meet in the street every day. People like them, they don't transplant. They just don't. My mother went to school with half of their street, as did my father. They all meet in church every Sunday, shop at the same vegetable stalls, insult the same butcher for having his thumb on the scales.'

'I envy them,' she says softly and, oddly enough, I believe her, even though the narrow world they inhabit would send her mad in a minute. Part of her wishes she could be satisfied with that, as does part of me. Then she turns to interrogating me. 'What is your dream? If you could have anything at all in this world, what would you have? Who would you be?'

I smile, as that is easy. 'I would have a café-bar. The sort of place that sits on a street corner, where there is simple food at a good price and decent beer. Where anyone can go and sit down and know that someone will talk to them, that they will feel comfortable. Whoever they are, whatever colour or creed. I'd love to run a place like that.'

'I can't cook,' she says. And we both laugh, as neither can I. 'Where?' she demands.

'No idea, but nowhere too sophisticated. I would want people to come whatever they wore, and whatever state of mind they were in. And feel safe.'

She leans forward and kisses my cheek, 'I could go for that,' she says, 'I could do the accounts.' And then she says, 'I told you about our last holiday in Barbados, how about there?' I shrug, it is all children's make-believe. I still believe Hohne has a bullet with my name on it. All I don't understand is why he hasn't fired it yet? But I feel far more reassured about Evie. He won't hurt her. Not yet, anyway.

The restaurant we have chosen is busy and noisy now, where it was quiet when we came in. I glance around. I am tired of daydreams. I have waited weeks for this woman, so I slide my hand up her thigh and rub a firm finger against the divide in her legs. Her breathy, 'Oh,' says everything I need to know. 'Home,' I say, and taking her hand, I tug her to her feet.

We are kissing as we stumble through my door. Evie reaches behind me and I feel the tips of her nails scratch my skin as she slides my tee shirt up my back. I keep kissing her, soaking up her flavour, as I undress her. As I had already scoped out her buttons and zips it takes moments and she is down to her panties so fast she looks giddy. I let her fumble over my belt buckle and zip. Feeling her hands tremble and struggle is pure delight as until she finally slides my trousers down my thighs. I kick them off and swoop her up in my arms and toss her onto the bed. I like doing that. I take a moment to unbuckle the knife and slide it under my pillow, and I am on to her.

Evie thinks she is ready for sex, but I disagree. Women rouse slowly, and the slower the rousing, the stronger their pleasure. She will fight me, but I am bigger than her, and that fact makes me grin. She is wearing cotton panties, which is perfect. Lace thongs are all very well as a turn on for men, but there are a zillion nerve endings between a woman's legs, and having them rubbed with the unevenness of lace is not what I want my woman to feel.

I slide my fingers, whisper soft, over her cunt. The cotton acts as a soft barrier, preventing my touch being too much. Nestled partly inside is her clit, but that is far too special to bring into play just yet. I part my fingers and slide along her moist lips, pressing against her precious clit, but not yet touching it. Evie's hips move of their own accord and I smile and kiss her hip bone. She murmurs my name, and her fingers convulse in my hair. I adore her fingers in my hair, pressing into my scalp, it is one of my favourite things. I ache for her, but control in this arena, as in so many, is key.

I keep soothing and rousing her by turns, and her hips are moving in deep circles, desperate for me to do more. She calls my name louder now, and it is a plea.

'Soon, princess,' I say. And concentrate harder. She is a musical instrument, at first I need to be certain of her low notes, and then lift the sound until we reach the climax. The top C of love making. I want to do this for her, I want it to be good. Now her hands are pulling at my hair and my grin widens and through the cotton I press two finger tips to her entrance. She begins to thrash, and my name is a constant litany, and she still has her panties on. I swirl and rub and press, then retreat to slide up the sides of her pussy. The soft, moist, sides of those lips press against her clit, and she moans. The fabric is damp, her hair tugging gets stronger and my grin gets even wider. When I am sure she is ready, I slide her panties down to her ankles and throw them away, only then do I slide two fingers inside her. She makes a high-pitched keening, and I begin to push in and out, and then I retreat, and only now do I slide my soaking finger-tips over her naked clit. She is thrashing now, so I push my fingers in again and then finger-fuck her hard and slow until she is close. The edge of her entrance has a mass of pleasure points and I make sure as I come out of her, I slide over just the right area. Evie calls my name over and over again and something inside of me sings in echo of the sound. Right now, she is my woman, mine, and it is me that is pleasuring her, only me. I can sense the beginning of her orgasm and lick and kiss her hips as I use my hand for her pleasure. She comes apart, jack-knifing almost in two as she cries out.

I move up her body and hold her close, and feel tears on my chest. I soothe her, stroking her back, whispering soft words into her hair, and keeping my groin well away from her. After a while I ask, 'Are you alright?'

She pulls away so she can look at me, her face wet. 'Oh my lovely Marco, until I met you, I thought I would only ever orgasm with a machine for the rest of my life. Thank you.'

As always, she says something I could never have predicted. Her honesty amazes me. 'And the tears?'

'Just an emotional release.' She begins to kiss my chest, pattering touches that make me even harder than I am. She finds my nipple and licks, then moves to my chest hair and shapes it into swirls with her tongue. It is my turn to groan.

'Evie,' I say, 'I am so hard I could break into a bank with my dick.' She giggles. Then one small hand grips me. My back arches off the bed and my groan is far louder than I intended. And then she licks the tip, sliding her tongue into the slit. 'Jaysus' I moan. Thirty-five years of trying not to blaspheme has just flown out of the window. Her hand is warm and now she is pulling up and down. I am losing it, fast. 'I want to be inside of you,' and it is my voice now that is pleading. 'Later,' she mumbles around me. I am trying not to thrust into her mouth, but to let her take only as much of me as she wishes. Nothing exists, there is no world, no universe, nothing, only Evie's warm mouth and my despera-tion. I have never felt so out of control. I fist my hand into her hair, not to force her onto me, but simply to touch her. I begin to buck uncontrol-lably. 'I am coming', I cry, expecting her to move away, but she tightens her grip on my thighs and stays with me. I pump into her mouth, and it is amazing. I have never done that before, never been with a woman who would do that. It is extraordinary to me how precious that feels. I feel accepted, cared for. I am a fool. But right that moment, an exhausted and contented fool.

She slides up my body and nestles in my arms, 'Good?' she questions.

'Foolish woman,' I say into her hair.

'Go to sleep,' she instructs and, I smile and do as she tells me. I tuck her tight into me. I move a hand to hold one of her breasts softly, knowing that as I sink into oblivion my hand will fall away, but for the moment, I want to claim her intimately as my own. My Evie. My woman. My love.

We make love when we awake in the early hours. And every moment feels precious. I hold her probably too tight when we once more slide back into sleep, but I cannot help myself. When we finally awake Evie, it seems, has been planning. She is enthusiastic, but I know we are building daydreams that can vanish as quickly a dainty soap bubble. But, I am free of work for a couple of days so we go and find a carpenter and decorator to repair the damage to her apartment. The police gave us a list of contractors and it seems that they are both competent and prompt. Once they are booked, she goes out furniture shopping while I go and hunt for a tall, thin, detective who appears to have heard of Hohne.

It is dark and raining when, finally, I see him leave his station and head for some form of transport home or perhaps some dinner. We are walking through people on a crowded pavement, the lights of cars and scarlet double-deckers moving past us on our left, bright shop windows on our right and small people with umbrellas poking our eyes out. London. A city I have come to love. As he waits at a crossing I lean forward and say softly in his ear,

'I think, Mr Policeman, you deserve a beer after a long day. I suggest you go and have one in The Kings Head, two streets away.' I melt backwards into the crowd as everyone pushes the other way to get across the road before the traffic begins again. He hesitates, dipping his head, and is barged a couple of times before he steps out and crosses briskly. He does not turn around. That, I think, is a good sign. I duck down an ally way, and head for The Kings Head in a different direction and in a hurry.

I arrive first. I can see him under the lights of a shop a few metres away, now searching around, his head constantly twisting. I step back into the shadows and wait. If he enters, I will follow him in, if not, I will have to think again. He does go in and sits at a table against the back wall positioned so he can watch the room. I go in, cross, and slide in opposite him.

'Thought it was you,' he says.

'I hoped you would.'

'What is this all about?'

'Hohne. Perhaps bringing him down.'

'Can't pretend that isn't what I was hoping you'd say.'

'But are you honest?' I ask.

His eyes narrow. 'Not sure what I should make of that remark.'

'Your partner, the one shorter than you, was wearing a silk tie. I recognised it. That tie cost what, a week's wages, two? How does a London copper afford such luxuries?'

'Perhaps more to the point, how does a criminal recognise a silk tie?'

'As it happens, I am not a criminal. And Hohne buys my work clothes, and he only shops at Saville Row and the like, even for paid-for thugs like me. He wanted me fitted for Lobb handmade shoes, but I insisted on something I could run in, rather than bespoke leather soles. He gave in on that, but grudgingly. He has a tie somewhat similar.'

'He spoils you.'

'Doesn't he just. We want to visit you, at your home, meet your family.' Might as well get Evie's idea right out there.

'My home? Stop taking the piss.'

'But I am serious. What we have in mind requires that we believe not just in your current honesty, but your future honesty.'

'You don't need to come to my home for that. I have been on the force for nigh on twenty-five years, and I have never taken a back-hander and never will. My colleague, Rhodes, is married to a male Saville Row tailor, as it happens. They don't have children, or a car, and spend their money on clothes and travel. Not that it is any of your business.'

'We will need more than your word.'

'Why?' He is suspicious, and I don't blame him.

'I have been researching into where the proceeds of crime go once a trial and so on is finished.' Actually, I haven't, but Evie has. 'It seems it goes to the police to cover some of their policing costs, the Crime Prosecution Service, who are the ones who decide when a case is worth processing, and local good causes. Which is all very well for a few hundreds or even thousands, but what about billions?' Well, that got his attention.

'What do you mean, billions?'

'Most people are fundamentally honest. I believe that. But give them a sniff of a billion pounds, and even a saint might get sticky fingers. If Evie and I can pull this off, we will relieve Hohne of his ill-gotten gains, and get him locked away for a very long time. If we don't do this, he is going to flit within the next few months.'

'Hang on, I am not keeping up. Why might Hohne do a flit?'

'Because he has commissioned a new yacht. It has a state-of-the art water purification system and two systems for generating energy, from either the sun or the sea. Basically, he will only have to touch land when he needs food. That thing is huge, it is a floating independent island. And he won't want for company, there are plenty of others owned by billionaires floating around the planet, beyond all reach of any kind of government or law.'

'Well, where are all these billions?'

'In banks, but we believe we can, shall we say, 'liberate' them. We will need to disappear forever and so we would like to keep one billion for ourselves. The rest we would like to place in a charity overseen by someone who will ensure that the funds help the communities Hohne has destroyed. Drug out-reach programmes, rehabilitation, helping the homeless, reintegrating the trafficked girls into society, mental health support, and so on. Men like Hohne get rich on destroying society. We don't trust the system that if it were given a huge sum of money it would have the skills and infrastructure to spend the money how it should be spent. Repairing some of the damage he has created.'

'Son, you are talking out of your backside. I don't believe a word of all this, and I have a nice, warm spot in front of my tv waiting for me. Oh, and my name is Goldington, not Mr Policeman.' He shoves his chair back and prepares to stand. Neither of us has got around to even ordering a pint.

'Ok, fair enough,' I say, 'but let me give you this. It won't help, I don't suppose, but it is factual.' I slide a piece of paper across.

'What is this?' Goldington leans forward and peers at the writing in the dim light.

'A date, exact time, location, of a crime involving arms. Too long ago now to be useful I expect.'

Goldington frowns at me and sits back down. 'Explain it to me.'

'I left my head office in Serbia for the UK hauling a manifest of engine parts. Was held up by a huge traffic snarl-up in France and arrived in the UK later than planned. Stopped at a service station for breakfast and a sleep. While I was eating a guy slid in next to me and shoved the barrel of a pistol in my side and told me to keep eating. I grabbed the gun, twisted it out of his grip breaking his wrist, and legged it out to my lorry. The customs seals had been broken and about twenty young people were being led out of the back of my lorry and being herded into two vans. When I ran towards them I was shot at. The bullet clipped a chunk of tarmac out of the surface of the lorry park. The guy from the café walked up, took his pistol back and they all drove away. Stuff from the back of my lorry had been heaped up on a piece of waste ground, had petrol poured on it and set alight.'

'And what did you do?'

'Headed back towards the Channel and found a farmer who let me park up for a few hours for a consideration so I could catch some sleep. I crossed the next morning and when I got back to my depot, was told that I now worked for Hohne. I said no and left to walk home. As I arrived in my street, a biker shot my younger brother once through the head. My mother caught him as he fell. Then my phone rang and I was told if I didn't comply, my mother and father would be next. At first I drove vans that I assume were full of something illegal, though I never saw what, drugs I presume, but when his personal driver was shot in some kind of altercation just outside Marseilles, I drove Hohne back to the UK and have been owned by him ever since.'

'Owned?'

'You think I can hand in my notice? He has my passport and although he pays me, he has access to my bank account so when he does away with me, he can simply empty it. And, he is effectively holding my parents hostage, and I love my parents.'

'And Ms Scott?'

'And that is where fear turns to terror. I feel guilt for every moment I spend in her company. If Hohne ever suspects we are a couple, he will have her followed or worse.'

Goldington looks at me and I know he is completely sceptical. 'Bugger off,' he says. Then, 'You still got the same phone?' I nod, and it looks as though our meeting is over.

I am half way home when my phone rings. I am walking, huddled from the rain down a side street. It is Goldington. 'Get back to the Kings Head.' A click, and it seems I have received my orders.

When I get back he has two beers on the table. Assuming one is for me I down it. I rarely drink, but dancing with the police can do that to a man. He taps the paper I gave him with a fingernail. 'This remains a live case.' I frown, not too sure what that means. 'Would you recognise the men who held up your lorry again?'

'You don't forget men who point guns at you,' I point out.

'No Mr Ilîc, quite the opposite. Most people would be so full of adrenaline due to panic and fear that they would remember very little of the whole incident. But an ex-soldier, now he might.'

I shrug, 'Well, I do.' Clearly Goldington has researched me, and I think a little more of him because of it.

'Your human cargo was arranged and 'owned' by Hohne, but the men who took those poor souls, were not his. They were hijacked by a team in the pay of a man called Carlos Xaviera, a drug baron based in Chile. We had been watching him when we came across Hohne. Hohne, however, is far more careful. He remains extremely hands on with his business, so it is much harder to find people who know anything about him. He keeps his teams small, and separate. Are you the only one who drives him?'

'Pretty much. I am off for a couple of days because of my knife wound, and he has cancelled all of his trips for the moment.'

'Exactly, he keeps knowledge as compartmentalised as possible. You are of value to him because one day he is going to want you to identify Xaviera's men. And, you know all about his business routes.'

'I did wonder why I am still alive. So, he believes I may have a use in the future and when he is ready, he will do away with me, and therefore wipe out anything I may have learned about his business.'

'Exactly.'

'Great.' My tone is sour, and what else can I say? I have always suspected something like this.

It is gone eight before I make my way back to Evie. The police tape has gone and two men in overalls are trotting down the stairs as I go up. Outside was a shiny grey van with fancy writing on the side. Evie has been spending money, at a guess. Her apartment is flooded with light and two guys are standing drinking coffee in her kitchen area. I try not to feel jealous, but it spikes my guts anyway. They are both about our age and good looking. I doubt either of them would ever work as a lorry driver.

'Marco!' I feel better as Evie's face lights up. 'This is Richard and Gary. They arrived back home to find the outer door broken when Lucas broke in and rang the police when they heard me scream.'

'Yeah, I am really sorry we didn't come up and see what was going on.' The blonde one looks guilty, the dark is eyeing Evie's breasts. I almost growl. Evie might find the noise amusing, these guys less so, I think. Dark one looks up and sees my expression, as does Evie.

'Thank you so much for all of your help,' she is saying, as they both edge past me and out of the door. She comes over and wraps her arms around me. 'You smell of beer, I didn't think you drank?'

I gather her in, pressing every inch of her against me. 'I don't often. I found Goldington. Who were those guys?'

'They live downstairs.'

'And they heard a woman scream, and did nothing?' I might have to pay them a visit and teach them a lesson. Evie is smiling up at me now,

'They have paid a penance. They came up when they heard the carpenter replacing the door and its locks. I suspect they were just being nosy, but I got them to help me to clear up and they took the sofa and armchair that had been slashed downstairs. From their grunts and groans and general bitching, I strongly suspect they found them heavy.' Her face is alive with laughter, so I kiss her to remind her I exist. She strokes my face, then unbuttons my damp coat. 'Would you like food or bed?'

'Bed,' I growl in her ear. Being a sensible woman, that is where we end up.

Afterwards, we sit up against the pillows in the warm glow of a lamp and eat Chinese brought by a delivery guy. I tell her about Goldington.

'I could do with access to Hohne's computer,' she muses.

'I know the first part of what his password was some time ago, but he might have changed it since then.'

'Really? People do not change their passwords nearly often enough.' She flexes her fingers theatrically, 'And they should to keep people like me out. What was it?'

'His name, Hohne, and then he went top left on the keyboard for three keys.'

She turns to gaze at me, eyes wide, 'Really? Then it will be Hohne123.'

'How can you know that?'

'Because he uses it as his first password into his Swiss bank accounts. There are a host of further protocols, but I know all of those as well.' She sounds so confident. Like a cat that has snagged a slice of meat from a forbidden plate she is decidedly smug. She is dangerous, I think, my Evie, in her own way.

Full of food, we snuggle down and check each other over for bruises and wounds. And that leads to more love making. I allow myself to doze a little, both sexually and gastronomically sated. She is safe, as for the moment am I, and life is good. It won't last, but it is a wonderful feeling.

I head back to my apartment at three in the morning. A far too chatty Uber driver drops me and accelerates off. I let myself in through the gate and climb up to my door. I enter and switch on the lights. I stand looking around, but I am too unsettled to go to bed, so go back down for a roam in the grounds. They aren't huge, this is central London and even billionaires cannot buy space that does not exist in a major city, but they are fairly extensive. The huge bushes, many taller than me, somehow make the space feel larger as walking in a straight line is almost impossible. My eyes are reaccustoming themselves to the dark when I smell cigarette smoke. I edge around a bush to see DePaul and Manon both sitting under an outside light. Only DePaul is smoking, and he bends to crush out the butt with his foot. I smile a little as he picks up the stub and puts it in his pocket. Hohne would not forgive cigarette butts in his grounds. It seems it is not only me who is cowed by the man. Then, my world upends itself. Manon reaches forward and places his hand around DePaul's neck. I tense, wondering if I am about to witness a murder, when Manon pulls DePaul closer and kisses him deeply. I step back carefully. This is not a scene I or anyone else is supposed to witness.

I have never practised walking silently with such concentration before as I wind my way back to my room. I cannot get my mind around what this might mean. Hohne is fiercely anti-gay. He spouts off about how all gays should be shot at dawn, or some such nonsense, fairly regularly. I ignore it. The man is a bigot, true, but he has bigger sins on his soul as far as I am concerned. But what might this mean about his security in the house? I always thought that the house was impregnable and that all of his security staff were completely loyal, but what I have just seen suggests that may not be the case. Considering how my mind is buzzing, I fall instantly deeply asleep.

My wounds pretty much healed I return to work. Where once my mind was blank as I worked for Hohne, now it churns constantly. Which addresses matter most to him? Who does he meet? How long for? I am now paying keen attention to his activities and am going to have to commit something to paper or screen soon as my memory is yelling it has too much to hold on to. I have always searched my apartment for listening devices but now I do so obsessively. Hesitantly, I belong to make notes on paper, but fear makes my hand tremble. My parents' lives hang on my keeping Hohne completely unaware of my new interest in him. Before I looked dumb because I was dumb; frozen into a state of compliance. Too 'stuck' to be able to think my way out of my predicament; waiting for him to finish me. Now, I have hope. Not much, but some. And whatever happens, he must not sense this.

When the car is once more spotless and ready to roll out of the garage in the service of its, and my, master, I head into the main house. Usually, I run and then work out in the gym, but this time I head into the kitchen with the hope that it will still be breakfast time. As I enter, only DePaul remains staring at his phone over a cooling mug of coffee. I walk to the machine and pour a cup for myself. To my back DePaul says, 'You don't usually come in here at this time of day.'

I swallow. All nine of Hohne's thugs are killers, but what the heck, now I am one of them. I close my eyes against the image of Lucas Wainwright lying in his own blood. I breathe deeply, and go to sit opposite DePaul. To my surprise he nods his head towards my left bicep.

'How's it doing? Healing?'

'Yeah, but it is a nuisance.' I grimace, 'I worked hard for my guns.'

He gives a grin, which to my surprise is not unkind. 'You should come and slob over in the rest room sometimes. Get into another fight and you might then have some support you could draw on.'

I stare into my coffee. 'I thought you had all been ordered to avoid me.'

'Yeah, but what the eye doesn't see the heart doesn't grieve over, hey mate?' He gives another good-natured grin and stands to leave.

'How long have you worked for him?' I ask, frowning.

'Nah then, you going to be a nark? Perhaps the boss is right, you are his little spy.'

'What?' I reach out and grip his forearm. 'What has he said about me?'

'That when he ain't here, you're his eyes and ears.'

I keep hold of his arm. 'No. No, no and no again. I have been terri-fied of coming into the house or mixing with you all as he said if I did one of you would 'end' me. I was to keep to myself or visit an early grave.' As DePaul seems to have changed his mind about leaving, I let go of his arm.

'Interesting,' he says. 'Clever git, Hohne.' And with that he is off.

I am left in the empty space to mull over his words. So, Hohne has had me separate in the garage apartment watching the house, and the house again separate, watching me. And never the twain shall meet. DePaul is right, Hohne is a clever bastard. It has worked for three long years. I finish my coffee and go back to put on my kit and go for a long run. I have a great deal to think about. I might not feel like venturing into the rest room with all of the others straight off, but I will begin to work-out in the gym when others are more likely to be there. And I will pass the time of day. Offer to assist on the weights. Who knows what I might learn? I shall tread carefully, I tell myself. Stepping into a nest of armed vipers is not to be hurried. As I pound the miles I wonder how good I will be at taking my own advice?

I am in the house gym working out that afternoon, lifting weights light enough on my left side not to rip my wound open, but pushing myself everywhere else. I have worked up a healthy sweat when three men walk in. Usually, I ignore them, continue working, then leave without saying anything. This time I place the weight down carefully and walk towards them. I hold out my hand,

'DePaul says I should say hello,' I say. One of the men is Manon, he drops his eyes and slides away unspeaking, but the other two take turns in shaking my hand. We quickly get into a discussion on lifts and weight regimes and I sense no animosity. Manon, however, remains at a distance. One of the guys says, 'You keep those bloody cars immaculate, man. It must be a dream to drive those limos.' From then on we are into

a deep discussion on high-end cars. After a while I realise that Manon
has stopped lifting but has drifted closer to listen. Eventually I say,

'I need to go and get ready to pick the boss up.' As I collect my
towel and water bottle and head for the door I give Manon a slight nod
and, to my surprise, he gives a small nod and smile back.

'Take care of that left arm, mate,' someone calls from behind me
and without turning I give a wave. Well, who could have predicted
that? Bored, underworked, and cut off from the outside world for long
dull hours at a time, it seems a new and friendly face is more than
welcome. They must be all heartily sick of each other. It is clear
DePaul has given me the nod, and I wonder whether he has an ulterior
motive and if so, what?

Later that night Evie's words make my hair stand on end. 'I need to
get into the house and access Hohne's computer,' she says as calmly as
if she is reading a menu. I stare at her. I don't even bother saying 'no',
she isn't going anywhere near Hohne and his lair. I have even
forbidden her to come to mine now she has given me a key to her place.
'Come on, Marco,' her tone is wheedling. 'You can get me in. I know
you can.'

'In, yes. But out, not so certain. And there are cameras everywhere
inside.'

'Cameras are only as good as the eyes looking at them.' I don't like
her smile. It is too knowing. 'Where are the screens, how often and how
conscientiously are they watched, and does anyone review data?' They
are all good questions. And I don't like the way I am being manipulated. She knows very well I would do anything for her. And that is a
thought I need to chew over some time. She hasn't finished. 'Is his
computer kept in his study and are there cameras in there?'

'Two.'

'But you know where they are?'

We are in her bed. We made love as soon as I arrived and the room
is covered in clothes thrown anywhere, anyhow. 'You are leading me by
my dick, aren't you.' My voice is flat. I am beginning to feel sick with
disappointment. Why am I really here? What can a brilliant woman

like Evie want with me? I am nothing. Evie climbs up onto her knees next to me and takes my face in her hands. I look into her eyes, and I know mine are sad. 'I should go,' I say. 'I will give Goldington what I can, but this fantasy has gone on long enough. Hohne is a killer. He is not a man you mess with.'

'Please don't go, not until you have to. I care about you, and I am determined to free you from his grip.'

I turn my head to one side, looking away from her.

'Marco, don't. Look at me.' She pulls my face around again so I am once more looking at her. 'Can't you see what you mean to me,' she whispers. I stroke my fingers through her hair, so soft, so full of golds and bronzes and nut browns. It slides across my big, work-roughened hands like satin. I stroke her skin, so soft and so blissfully comforting when I hug her close. She has come to be the reason I breathe, but am I being a fool?

'I don't understand what you see in me,' I admit.

'I see a wonderful, loyal, man who is trapped in a situation not of his making. I see a kind and patient man. I see a man who makes my legs go weak when he kisses me.' She smiles, and I am comforted. Just a little. She leans in and kisses me, and I can taste the yearning. Is the yearning for me, or for Hohne's fortune? She sits back.

'Ok,' she says briskly, 'I need to explain more of why I am so determined to bring Hohne down.' She pulls on my tee shirt and settles it over her thighs. I shove another pillow behind my head and sit more upright. 'Money today is as powerful as it ever was, but it is in fewer hands. The rich are richer than anyone has ever been, and the result is that globally, everyone else is doing not just less well, but in some places, truly suffering. After the second world war, the allied powers laid down rules that money had to remain within geographical barriers so that it was subject to laws and oversight. From 1950 to 1970 all economies flourished and there were no recessions. That has all gone. Partly as a result of the dollar no longer being linked to gold and partly as a result of the London financial market deregulating. Simplifying, these two actions overturned what had been the status quo.

'Money will always find the gaps where one law does not mesh fully with another. It is in those gaps that money can flow. Does this matter? Yes. It is patently unfair that a working person pays more tax as a ratio of earnings that a company. A self-employed plumber, for example, who is also a business, will pay more pro-rata than a global company with a profit sheet in the millions.

'Nowadays people as rich as Hohne live outside of both geography and law. He is currently building a yacht that will give him an independent island to live on. I doubt the flow of money to the uber-rich can be stopped but I am determined to re-direct at least one fortune to the kind of causes it should be spent on. Ordinary people, in other words.'

'That's a massive ambition,' I say. I feel both sick with fear for her and slightly excited. Her confidence is seductive. As are her boobs.

'We can do it Marco, I know we can. You can give the police information about Hohne, enough to have him locked up, and when that happens, I will quietly syphon his money and put it elsewhere.'

'Switzerland?'

'Heavens no, Nevada probably.'

'What, in the United States?'

'Mm. The best places to hide money are all in the US now. Long story, I could go on for hours, but basically the US has enough muscle to ensure banks around the world give them information but they don't reciprocate. This means, that money placed in certain US banks is completely invisible. It can belong to crime lords, those who fear crimes such as kidnapping if anyone knew what they were really worth, and those who fear their own governments for whatever reason.' She frowns, 'Yup, I think those are the three main groups. There are also politicians who have robbed their own exchequers and want to move the money so when they leave power they can live wild and free, while their populations struggle without the infrastructure that money was raised for.'

I frown at her. 'You really do believe in all this, don't you?'

'Passionately. I spent four years working out how to make rich people richer and was awarded a serious academic honour for it. And now I want to turn that knowledge upside down and use it against the uber-rich. Money is limited, and should do good. Not just buy huge yachts and luxury jets. Most people seem to find the super-rich fascinating. I see them as immoral.'

'But don't the rich just by existing offer a dream of possibilities to ordinary people? When they are shown off in glossy magazines, they say, hey, life can be colourful and wonderful, and people love that.'

'How many cars do you groom for Hohne?'

I grin and shake my head, 'Seven.'

'And how many does he need?'

'One.' I can't help but laugh, and slide my hands up her sides under the tee shirt. 'This is mine,' I say, 'and I want it back. I need to drill some sense into my little communist.'

'Rational capitalist,' she insists, but she is wriggling as I tickle her. She falls to one side and is now laughing and swatting my hands away. The tee shirt comes off and I pull her in to feel her wonderful softness close. Her warmth heats me and she slides a hand between my legs.

'Mm,' she murmurs, 'seems all this talk of money turns you on.'

'Nah, it's you who turns me on,' and I kiss her deeply. She has come to mean so much to me. Her laughter and her touch have broken me out of my invisible cage. Part of me worries I care too much. The other part says, 'What the hell.'

Rather than call an Uber I walk through the dark streets as dawn streaks the sky. I can catch up on my sleep later while I wait for him. Being cocooned in the hand-sewn leather of the Bentley he has taken to using isn't a bad place to doze. I smell of Evie, of her sex and her perfume and my body is relaxed and sated. She is the first woman I have considered having a serious relationship with, and she is as mad as a hatter. Take on Hohne? On the other hand, I have believed from day one that he has a bullet with my name on it, so what have I to lose? I shake my head, it won't work, but it might be fun. As long as I can keep little Evie safe.

· · ·

The Driver

I meet Goldington in a different pub to The Kings Head. Just in case we were spotted before. Evie's mum is fading. She had left for Felixstowe and I don't know when she will be back. Her not being around has left me feeling lost, which is odd. For three years I have trotted through my days without much emotion, but now I am restless and definitely out of sorts. I need some action; to be doing something.

'What do you know about Carlos Xaviera?' I ask Goldington. He is in mufti, which for him means baggy jeans and a stripy woollen jumper. He looks like a dad out for his annual pint with a mate.

'Why do you want to know?'

His suspicion reaches across the table like a physical presence. 'Keep your hair on. I wish to follow him a little, learn more about him. Where he goes, who he meets, what his business is.'

'He is a dangerous man.'

I laugh at that. 'Yeah, and my employer is a sweet daisy picker.'

He gives a nod at that. 'Fair dos. What have you got for me?'

I pass over a notebook. I started off writing in print to disguise my handwriting, but gave up as I had so much to impart. Goldington begins to read. I drink my soda and lime and watch a pretty girl flirt with a dark-haired lad two tables from where she is sitting with her mates. He should get lucky tonight. A snog at least looks to be on his cards.

Goldington's voice cuts into my musing. 'Crikey mate, this is a goldmine. I thought you said you didn't know much?'

'Didn't think I did.'

'Tell me again why you want to know about Xaviera.'

'Just curiosity. You said he robbed Hohne of his cargo three years ago. I wondered what kind of business he is in, whether it overlaps with Hohne's. I rather like the idea of Hohne having competition, or,' I pause and shrug, 'someone out to get him.'

'Steady on, I don't want a gang war stirred up on my patch.'

'Nor do I. I am the one most likely to be caught in the crossfire. I just want to snoop around a bit.'

Goldington stares at me a long time. I sit quiet and gaze back at him. Eventually he says, 'There is a pub called The Three Elms in Wandsworth. He seems to be based there. But stir up any gangland stuff and I might be the one to shoot you; you won't have to wait around for Hohne or Xaviera.'

I grin and down my drink. 'Good to know.' I stand and leave him there, still turning the pages in my notebook.

London is a series of villages, all now knitted into what we know as the modern city. Knightsbridge, where Evie and I both live, has been posh pretty much for ever. Wandsworth has always been different to rarefied Knightsbridge. It hosts a huge prison that revolves into public consciousness with regularity when it is hit by yet another scandal. The area was on the up for a while, then it was hit by Covid and the recession. Now it is choc-a-block with the low-paid, who despite working flat out, have little to look forward to. So, perhaps not surprising it is fertile ground for men like Xaviera. If a man has no future, he will search for one. Just look at me.

I go in daylight the first time, getting there by bus and walking. I want to get a decent feel for the area. I walk around, buy a paper, sit in cafés. The Three Elms is a nice looking place, all Victorian glass windows outside and polished brass here and there. A big guy in a tracksuit lounges against the corner of the brickwork. He fiddles with his phone and every so often glances up and down the street. He doesn't fit the rather smart look of the place, with his gut hanging out and his need to repeatedly pull up his trackie bottoms. A couple of men in business suits walk up and enter, but not before both of them give a frowning glance at the big sloppy-looking guy. Lunch time, but although I am hungry, I will not be eating alongside them in The Three Elms.

I drift around the area some more, and then head back. Hohne surprises me by finishing work by eight that night, so I slip out quietly and head back to Wandsworth. By ten, I am tucked up in an alcove, unmoving, diagonally opposite The Elms. At eleven, five men emerge. I have never seen Xaviera, but who else would wear mirrored shades on a dark, drizzly night, surrounded by four oiks? I stay so still I am hardly breathing. Movement catches the eye, stillness is ignored. My hoodie is up shading my face from any light cast by passing cars and soaking up the drizzle rather than let it dribble down my neck. I study the four men, not the man I assume is Xaviera. Fat guy is there, now dressed in a cheap suit. He doesn't look any smarter. The other three don't look anywhere except at the big, shiny, black SUV that pulls up to collect them. I have now attended two personal security courses and have the certificates to prove it. Mama would be real proud of her boy. But at least I know enough to keep my eyes going everywhere. These guys, nada. They are oblivious to everything. I could swing out my gun and take all five out before they knew what was going on. Madness. He could save himself a pile of money and not bother with them. Three climb into the car and it pulls away, while fat guy stands and watches them depart. Then, his head low, he wanders back into the pub.

My night is over. I wait for a while, just to let the street settle down and confirm that there is no danger to me around, and then I walk away towards the nearest Tube station. The drizzle has not let up and I decide to call an Uber. The way the weather is going I am going to be soaked through if I do much more walking. I am picked up at the end of the street and settle back to be chauffeured for once. We have been going for about ten minutes when I spot a car I recognise. I lean forward and tap the driver on the shoulder, 'Hey mate, can you pull in a minute, I think I recognise someone I know.' He jams the car against the curb on double yellows and I slide out, 'Don't go anywhere, I just need a quick look.'

I hurriedly jog back down the street and check the number plate, and yes, it is the vehicle Xaviera got into. I trot back to the Uber. 'Thanks mate,' I say, 'I'll give you a good tip for that.' As we drive away I find Goldington's number on my phone. I have entered him as 'Betty' just to wind him up if he ever finds out. He answers just as I am beginning to think he might be asleep; it is nearly mid-night by now.

'What's up?' he asks.

'I think I have seen Xaviera. Medium height, dark hair, longish around his ears, dark shades at night, escorted by four thugs.'

'If he was coming out of the Firs, sounds possible.'

'Yeah, but is where he has gone next that is important. He is inside the fourth address in my notes, the one on the edge of Wandsworth. There is a taxi company below, shall we say 'managed' by Hohne, and the rooms upstairs are all his.'

'The brothel?'

I glance at the Uber driver, but I haven't said much and he can't hear Goldington, so his blank expression is probably genuine. 'Yeah.'

'Why the hell would Xaviera go into one of Hohne's places?'

'Um, you know what you were afraid of in the pub?'

'Oh shit. Do you think Xaviera is starting to try to muscle Hohne about?'

'That's your area of expertise. I am just worried.'

'Yeah, now there are two of us. Thanks for the intel.'

And he is gone. I sit back and watch the rain hit the side windows of the car. Gang war. No one wins and lots end up dead. What a great plan, Xav my man. Do you think Hohne will sit around and let you pay little visits to his palaces?

Back at my apartment I pace. My phone pings and it is Evie.

Can't sleep. Miss you. X

I ping back, Miss you too. Stay safe. How is your mum?

Evie: They say tomorrow. I just want her to be at peace now.

Me: I will be here when you need me.

Should that have been an 'if'? Am I taking too much for granted, but her reply settles me.

Longing for one of your hugs. Night night my lovely man. Xxx

The message from her, and the kisses, settle me down. I ache for her. And I am desperate to keep her safe. The fears I have about messing with Hohne flood in and I spend a restless night.

In the morning I am standing by the car as usual. Half way down the steps he stops and peers at his phone. He tenses, and so do I. He stands for a moment staring at the garden out over the clipped topiary his mind clearly elsewhere. What was Xaviera up to last night? At least Evie is miles away with her mother at the moment. I can tell when he comes to a decision, and he continues towards me and goes to slide into the Bentley. It is on the tip of my tongue to check that it is still number 22 that we are going to, but bite down hard on the question. I am the dumb driver. I am not ever astute. Control. All my life is control. Give nothing away has been my mantra for a long, long time.

As we slide through the London traffic I use my mirrors to watch Hohne. Every time I look he is staring blankly out of the side window. I don't need my excursion from last night to tell me something is wrong. I stop on double red lines and step from the car to walk around to the pavement side and hold the door for Hohne. I am wearing mirrored shades just like Xaviera. With my perfectly tailored suit sliding over my muscles I look exactly what I am. An upmarket thug bodyguard. Just what Hohne wants me to be. And as I turn to click the door shut and move through the press of traffic I wonder what Evie sees when she looks at me. The thought worries me enough for me to shove it out of my mind.

I slide into a bus stop to park and ring Goldington. 'Hohne has altered his plans. I was to pick him up at two, now he wants me at eleven. Something is bothering him.'

'Good to know.'

'By the way, I am parked up in a bus stop; make sure I don't get a ticket will you? If I do, Hohne will want to know why I stopped.' I put the phone down on his swearing. I am grinning as I turn to pull back out into the almost solid traffic, but as I do so, an SUV with plates I recognise slides past me, forced on by the vehicles around it. Xaviera? Is he following me? Or Hohne? Goldington says that this isn't 1930s Chicago, so we won't be having tommy-guns at dawn, but I am beginning to worry.

Back at the house I clean the car and go for a run. I am so tense with wondering what will happen next I need to unwind. When I get back I go for food and a coffee in the main kitchen. DuPaul is there chatting to Carla, the housekeeper. He seems to spend a lot of time in there. I have rarely come into the house and not found him.

'Jeez, look at you,' he swings his coffee mug towards me.

I pull the bottom of my tee shirt up and wipe my dripping face with it. 'Yeah, I need to cool down. Any coffee on the go Carla?'

'Of course, come, I bring you one over.'

I take the coffee gratefully and wander, as if I am simply walking aimlessly, out of the kitchen and into the corridor. I drift until I am outside of the 'guardroom'. It is where the screens are for all of the cameras that are around the place, along with comms equipment that goes in and out as required. I lean on the doorframe and sip my coffee. There are two men inside, only one of whom I recognise. He looks up.

'Donner,' I say, with a nod.

'Wanker,' he answers, and I grin. We aren't blood brothers yet, but it is a start. He and the other guy are using one of the screens to play 'Assassin's Creed'. I bet they don't know that the game is based on a novel by a Slovenian. Not a Serb, I shrug, but a kinda cousin. Possibly. What is clear is that Donner is winning and that neither are watching any of the other screens. Having learned something, I mosey on. I wander into Hohne's office and stand in the middle of the floor looking around, but touching nothing. There are two cameras in here that cover pretty much the whole room. If Hohne says anything about me standing in the middle of his carpet dripping sweat and sipping coffee, that too will tell me something. I drain my mug, and turn and wander out again and head for the gym and some weights.

I have finished and feel good. My left bicep is still healing, it aches, but in a good way. As I stand and push my arms above my head to stretch out my spine DuPaul comes and sits on the weights bench beside me. I glance down at him. Then ignore him, bending my spine to each side.

'How's the arm?' he asks.

'Better.'

'I heard it was a deep one.'

'Yeah, the guy put his whole body-weight behind it.'

I look down at the top of DuPaul's head. 'Want something?' I ask.

He has his elbows on his knees and is staring at his dangling hands.

'What has Hohne got on you? He keeps you separate 'cos you aren't like us, are you? I bet you don't have one prison tat.'

'No, no I don't. I am really just a lorry driver. A good one. But just a lorry driver.'

'Ahh,' he sighs. 'I have two prison tats and I don't want a third.'

I don't say anything. How any of us can guarantee staying out of prison when we work for Hohne beats me. I begin to wipe down the equipment I have used.

'See,' says DuPaul, 'that's what I mean. Most of the other blokes don't bother doing that. They come from homes where the idea of a cleaning cloth is as alien as an actual alien. Let alone consideration for someone else.'

'What do you want to know?' By now I have my towel and water bottle and am ready to leave.

DuPaul is still looking away. 'What's he got on you. Why are you here?'

I stare at the top of his head and realise that his hair is thinning. He will have a bald spot soon. 'Why do you want to know?'

He swivels to look up at me. 'Just wondering.'

I scratch an ear. 'Put it this way. I didn't answer a job ad.' With that I walk away. But once again I am wondering, how many of Hohne's men are really loyal to him? I have a suspicion DuPaul isn't, and if he isn't, from what I saw, Manon won't be either.

At eleven I pull up outside 22 Bishopsgate, walk around and stand on the pavement and by the back passenger door. All around me traffic hoots and drivers gesticulate. I stand still and straight and ignore it all. As far as I know, Hohne has never once been fined for the use he makes of London's double reds. I need to warn Goldington. Hohne definitely has police on his payroll. I wonder, just for a heartbeat if Goldington is one of them. At that moment, Hohne appears, slides in without a word, and I edge out into the traffic.

As I finally edge into a space half the width of the Bentley in between a taxi and a Porsche, Hohne gives me an address. I bite into the inside of my mouth, hard. Control, I tell myself, no reaction, never make a reaction. The address is the brothel and taxi place I saw Xaviera go into. When we arrive, I park behind the line of taxis.

'Do you want me to move closer and double park?' I ask. We usually arrive at mid-night when most of the taxis are at home with their drivers.

'No, I will walk from here.'

Control. Don't smile. It must be all of twenty metres. The traffic isn't as intense here as it was outside 22, and I slide out and walk around to open his door for him without a delay. Again I have donned the mirrored shades. Got to look the part.

'I come with you?' I ask. When we have come here before I have always waited in the car.

Hohne gives me a disparaging look. I should have said, may, or do, or would you like that, or a dozen other words in front of my question. It is more a Serbian phraseology, and I am more aware of when I do it now Evie has pointed it out. And now I am aware, I can use it so that Hohne will give me a look exactly like that. I am his dumb driver. Nothing more. Too cowed to think for myself.

He gives a sniff, and strides off. It would make a rather marvellous photograph, I think. The ultra-smart businessman, with his limousine and immaculate bodyguard behind him, striding into a seedy taxi office in a run-down part of a major city. What might I title it? The haves and the have nots? Perhaps. I remain outside of the car, watching. I want to see Hohne behind bars, not mugged in Wandsworth; and nor do I want the limo scratched by some idiot with a set of keys and a death wish.

He comes out about fifteen minutes later and is clearly furious. His face is red, his fists knotted white by his thighs and his stride hurried. I open the door as he reaches me and move around to pull the car away.

'Home,' he snaps.

I risk a question, 'Trouble boss?'

He stares out of a side window and doesn't answer, and I kick myself.

I am laid off for the rest of the day and flick a quick text to Golding-ton: Hohne pissed after visit to taxi office Wdswth.

His message in reply is: Pissed is US. Pissed off is UK.

I send him a picture of a hand with one finger raised. I am beginning to like Goldington. Evie is due back today and so I also text her to ask when I can call around. The one-word reply galvanises me: Now

I am at her door within twenty minutes. When she opens it I know I have never seen anything more lovely. Her hair is loose falling in soft waves around her shoulders and she is dressed in a tee shirt with loose jogging bottoms. Her feet are bare and her toenails are a pretty pink. Like little seashells. And then the cherry on the cake, she says,

'I have missed you so much.'

I don't need a second invitation. I step inside and kiss her with all of the longing and loneliness I have bottled up inside. And the lust, of course. Eventually I let her go a little and ask,

'Talk, coffee, or bed?'

'Bed,' is the answer I am hoping for and the one I get.

Evie is different this time. I mean, I think lovemaking is always different, every time. To me it is a kind of chemistry, and the ingredients are always a little varied. Perhaps that is what makes it so addictive. Or perhaps it is just pleasure centres in the brain. Whatever it is, Evie is different. Fiercer, more needy, less guarded. I try to go slow but she is on fire. When she buries her teeth deep into the area beside my neck, I get the message and go for a straight-forward fuck. She seems to approve. As we both finish, she curls into me and begins to cry, then the crying turns to heart-breaking sobs. I hold her close and want to take everything away and wrap her in cotton wool. But of course, I can't and shouldn't. Life is for living. I murmur soft words instead, calling her sweetheart and precious, wondering if she will ever care enough about me to know that I am giving her my heart with every whisper.

Eventually, she pulls away. 'Sorry,' she says, attempting to wipe her face. I stop her and mop her gently with the bedsheet.

'No need to sat sorry, you have just buried your mother.' I drop a kiss on her brow now that the tears have stopped.

'I don't want to talk about it,' she says looking away.

'Wouldn't it be better to tell me?' I press.

'I'll make coffee,' she says. Then, she slides out of bed and pulls my tee shirt over her head. I love the way she takes possession of my clothes. She wears a French perfume called Arpége. I have bought her a big bottle in the hopes we will still be together by Christmas, which isn't too far away now. I am still tracking down a matching body lotion and soap on the internet, but have had no luck so far. But, I still have a number of weeks to go. I breathe in deep and can find the scent on the sheets and on me. Many perfumes that women spray themselves with smell harsh to me, but Evie's is soft and feminine. I fully support her surrounding herself in this one. Some others make my throat sore. I am musing on nothing more than this when she abruptly says,

'It was so hot. I hated it. Everyone was uncomfortable. And hardly anyone came. Just the nurses from the home and one or two others. She had been out of her life for so long.' Then she turns and heads to the coffee percolator. I slide a thumbnail through the gap in my front teeth thinking. Outside early Autumn leaves are beginning to swirl around and I wore a jacket over here. 'Out of her life for so long.' The words hang in the air. I have been out of my life for over three years. Not as poor Evie's mum was, with her body not knowing that her mind had gone. But still, I have been living a void life. And Evie has brought me back to sensation and the wish to move on, somewhere, anywhere. I can no longer stay an automaton.

When we are settled in with coffee, warm and for the moment physically sated, Evie shatters my pleasant drifting mood entirely.

'We will need at least four false passports,' she says. When all I do is stare at her, my mind blank, she adds, 'For our escape.'

'Escape?' I mutter.

'As I see it, the only way we can disappear is to leave this country under assumed names so that no one knows that we have left. Then in this intermediary destination, change our looks and then exit that country for where we really want to go, again under false names.'

'And where do we get false passports?' I ask. I mean, they aren't exactly stocked by our local supermarket.

'I am hoping Goldington knows some crooks. I mean, the police do, don't they? Know crooks?'

'More than they probably want to,' I say. It is beginning to dawn on me that this might not actually be a day dream, but something that might happen. In my mind, my helping Goldington with information about Hohne had nothing to do with Evie's mad plan.

'Barbara has done a load of research.'

'Barbara'? Who is Barbara?

'Mrs Goldington. She is a senior nurse and is researching charities that she thinks look interesting. She has also come up with a plan for asking health professionals she knows to join a new organisation to help with first the girls who have been traded and prostituted and then the drug addicts. Both groups would need an awful lot of support.'

An understatement if ever I heard one. 'When did you speak to her?'

Evie's brows raise. 'Oh, we have been on video. She is really excited.'

'What exactly have you told her?'

'I just asked that if I gave her a stupendous amount of money, did she want to spend the rest of her life making it work for something better than big yachts, fast cars and botox for blonde girlfriends? And she said yes.'

I open my mouth and close it again. 'It is stealing, you know.'

Evie gives me a straight look. 'I do know that, Marco. It is just that Barbara and I don't care.'

'And what if it goes wrong? What if you end up getting arrested?'

'I will crowd-fund a decent barrister.'

I find I have nothing to say. My mind is simply not coping with what she is planning. A palm, warm from hugging her coffee, is laid against my cheek. 'Stop worrying, Marco. We can do this.' She reaches forward and lays heated, coffee tasting lips on mine. At first I find that my mind has short-circuited my body, than normality returns and I tug her down and roll on top of soft luscious curves. Perhaps I can seduce this madness out of her. I can only hope.

Walking home it is her final comment that bangs around my brain. Apparently for all this to work, Evie needs access to Hohne's home computer. That, I am not happy about. What is more, I am now certain that I am being used. The question is, do I mind?

The afternoon with Evie has soothed and rattled me in equal parts. It is now late. Hohne is still out-of-sorts. As on so many other nights, I drive him around his various pick-up points where he meets with his drug suppliers or checks on his brothels. I have to admit the man works for his money. But from the bags that go into the boot sometimes, he is doing well from his efforts. Our last stop is the brothel and taxi rank that Xaviera visited. Hohne has me carry a heavy holdall over to the taxi office. As I drop it on a desk the row begins. It is clear that the guys there are not happy about the amount of cash Hohne is laundering through them. I step outside, but remain close. I may wish someone would put a hole into the man, but if that happens, perhaps Mama and Tata would be targeted; I have no idea what plans he has in place.

From a door to my left two girls emerge. They are both young and stick thin. One lights two cigarettes, takes a dragged breath on both, then passes one to the other girl. The night is cold, but they are wearing tiny skirts with bare legs and pin-thin high-heels. Wrapped around their middles are bands of stretchy cloth that only just covers their small breasts. They both draw deep, making the fire at the end of the tubes flare with a hot light. I suspect nicotine isn't the only drug that they are hooked on.

Hohne steps out and heads towards me and the car. The girls spot him and one steps forward, calling something I don't hear properly. As she moves into the lighted doorway of the taxi place I can see that she is horribly young. She reaches out for Hohne and places a hand on his chest, just under the silk handkerchief that peeks out of his top pocket. Her body language shouts that she has been intimate with him, and from the looks of it, the poor girl has feelings for him. The sound of the slap he gives to her face echoes from the blank walls around us, despite the constant growl of a major city late at night. She staggers backwards.

Her crying is all the more poignant because it is silent. The tears run like molten gold in the cheap yellow of the taxi office lights.

While he gives her a hissed lecture, I turn away. Rage roars inside of me. A rage I didn't know I could still feel. In Chechnya, when I was ordered to blast people's homes apart, health centres, schools, I felt the same impotent rage. I breathe deep. Hohne must not see how much his behaviour has flicked my switch. And I might not be impotent now. Evie has a plan. And Evie needs help. I will give her everything I have. And if I told them everything, Mama and Tata would most likely support me. Tata hates bullies. Despises thugs. And despite the Saville Row bespoke suit and the handmade shoes, that is what Hohne is. They are no longer young. And God forgive me, but I am going to put their lives to one side and take Hohne down if I can. I will be black-mailed by their lives no longer.

As we drive back to the house I breathe through my nose, determined not to show how much my inner life has changed. Hohne is preoccupied, but not by the girl, I think. As soon as I am free, I slide silently down the fire escape out of my apartment and go to wake Evie. When she opens the door I say,

'I want to do it. Tell me what you need.' She says nothing, only pulls the door wider and goes to her phone. Without a word to me she presses a button and I hear the sharp sound of the phone ringing. When it is answered she says, 'Can we come over. Now.'

Goldington and his wife were clearly asleep when we rang. As it is past one in the morning, that is hardly surprising. They both have demanding jobs. Evie takes over immediately.

'Who do you know who can forge passports to a decent standard?'

'No one,' Goldington frowns. Which is where Mrs Goldington, Barbara, takes over.

'If you don't know, who will?'

'GCHQ,' he mutters. Yeah, I think, the UK security service most certainly can, but they are unlikely to help us.

'We need four to begin with,' Evie says. 'Two for us and two for Marco's parents.' I turn and frown at her. What have Mama and Tata to do with this? She adds, 'I intend to go to Serbia and ensure that they are far away under different names before we begin the take-down.'

The take-down, I think. Is that what robbing an evil man is called? 'You can't go to Serbia,' I say, 'you don't speak Serbian. And why would they do what you say?'

'Because you will give me enough information to prove to them that I come from you, and your Mama speaks quite a bit of English.'

'Does she?' I mean, does she?

'Your auntie taught her and she has been going to classes. She says learning English is a way of touching her son, you.'

'How do you know that?'

'I follow her on Facebook.'

Evie now ignores me and begins to hound Goldington. Barbara joins in. He hasn't a hope. It turns out that he might know a man who might know a man. 'Money is no object, secrecy is,' Evie says. We leave with a promise that Goldington will make the attempt. He is muttering, 'Twenty-five years a copper.' Barbara is sniffing and saying, 'And how often have you watched evil men get away with their crimes or get insignificant sentences during those years? I do listen to your grumbling, you know.' We slide out of the kitchen door and leave them to it.

'I can't do anything until your mum and dad are safe,' Evie is muttering. I was smitten before, but now I am in even deeper. Family is everything to me. Mama, Tata, my brother in Germany. Grief kicks like a wild horse. My little brother. The motorcycle mechanic. The joker. The teaser. Always with a grin on his face. And if I had said yes to Hohne immediately, he would still be alive. The Uber we have called arrives to take us back to Evie's. I stare out of the side window all the way there. I can feel her gaze on my face, but I cannot turn to look at her.

On the pavement outside her apartment she reaches for my arm. 'Marco,' she says softly. 'Are you getting cold feet?'

'No. Every day I drive him with a gun and a knife strapped to me. Why haven't I simply killed him before now?' My voice sounds strange in my ears.

124

'You know why,' Evie says softly.

'I should have said yes. If I had just said yes, my brother ...' I can't go on.

'Ah Marco, have you ever grieved for him?'

The answer is of course, no. I couldn't face it. The sound of the shot, him falling like a stringless puppet, the blood, my mother's wail, the space he left in the world. Because of me.

'Come inside Marco, let me hold you.'

'No, I have to go.' She pulls on my arm.

'Please Marco, stay. Let me comfort you as you have comforted me.'

I shake my head, give her a brief hug, and walk away, heading back to my pristine room. Perhaps I will break one day. But not today. And if I stay, I will break. I need my walls back in place. And I will not give in to the stranglehold tears have on my throat. My walk becomes a jog, which becomes an outright run. Control, my mind chants.

It takes four days. Just four days. Money, it seems can buy anything, and Evie has sufficient. She flies to Serbia the Thursday after our meeting with the Goldingtons with the forged passports for my parents and is back by the Friday night. In less than a week since we planned this my parents are in possession of false documents and have been persuaded to travel to Canada for a tour. Mama and Tata, not just leaving Serbia for the first time ever, but taking their first real holiday. Evie has found a number of Serbian families who have settled in Canada and come across a couple who are about the same age as Mama and Tata and are willing to meet them at the airport and tuck them under their wing. Evie's organisational skills leave me amazed and impressed, and I begin to believe we might just pull this off. This take-down.

Evie is jubilant, and when I meet her at her apartment climbs my body like a monkey. I hold her easily and swing her around, both of us now laughing. Her joy is infectious. I tumble her onto the bed and we make up for the nights we lost. I pound into her with a touch of desperation. If her plan works, I assume that will be the end of us. And I don't want it to end. As we lay gasping and spent she strokes my face.

'I see, sex then news about your family.'

I give a rueful smile. 'I missed you.'

'So I see.'

'Did you mind?'

Her face takes on a tenderness I rarely glimpse and she cups my face gently and gives me a sweet, small, kiss. 'No,' she says, and her voice is husky. Then she is all business.

'I loved them. Your Mama's English is rough, but we could get by. I did a lot of hand-waving, diagram drawing, and I learnt the word for tea. Caj.' I grin, correcting her pronunciation. How can one three letter word be spoken with an English accent? 'But we only drank coffee, 'Kafa'. And your mother never stopped pressing food on me. She just didn't. At the moment, I feel I need to starve for a week to recover!'

'Ah, that sounds like my Mama. Are they both well?'

'Apart from being worried sick about both you and your brother, yes, very well. They seem solid, sufficient people, and I mean that as a compliment. They aren't the sort to wilt easily.'

My grin widens, no, wilt is definitely a term I could never envisage using in terms of my Mama or Tata. 'When will they head to Canada?'

'The end of next week. I need to get in to see Hohne's home computer as soon as they are safe.'

'How will we know?'

'The hosts have agreed to put a message on their Facebook page to say that the two roaming horses have been safely stabled.'

'Roaming horses?'

'There are nearly as many horses as people in their village.' Her tone is condescending, making me grin again. I like the idea of a village. I hope that means that they will be safer and more comfortable than in a modern city. My home town is poor and the mesh of streets where I grew up is more like a village than the urban town it is supposed to be.

Chapter Eight

The week passes slowly. Hohne's temper appears to improve, and then on the Friday he tells me he will not need me until eight on the Saturday night. He had done this before. He meets friends for dinner at a hotel. I know that hotel. There is an exclusive nightclub in the basement and he and his friends will migrate there and he will not want picking up until the early hours. I tell Evie that she is to have her chance.

I have spent the week roaming the main house at odd hours. I have drifted past the camera screen room several times, often lounging on the door frame and watching the computer games, groaning or grunting a cheer as the players win or lose. About half of the guys give me a nod or the time of day, while the other half don't speak but simply glare at me, still convinced I am a spy for Hohne. The most aggressive is a guy called Dunbar. I have tried to send a slight friendly nod his way, but he makes it clear he would rather rip my head off. Well, I reason, he can try. I don't give much for his chances, though.

I am tight with nerves on the Friday. Mama and Tata are safely tucked away in Canada, my brother has disappeared into Germany and if Hohne finds him, well, he will have done better than I have, but there is still little Evie. The thought of anything happening to her rips my guts apart.

'Why can't I go in and do this?' I hiss at her one more time.

'Don't be such a lump. What do you know about computer files?'

She has a point. And if Evie does it, we can get it over in one go. If I go in and mess it up, we could be in a far worse state than we are now, with Hohne on the warpath.

'There is a utility cupboard. Carla keeps the vacuum and mops in there, and there is no camera inside. I will put you in there and then see how clear the coast is.'

'Marco, you have told me this a dozen times. Stop worrying.'

But I can see that she is shaking slightly. I am glad she is not too confident. It is good to be a little nervous, I think. Me, I am worried out of my head that she might be hurt.

We move as quietly as possible through the shrubbery that leads from the back gate to the pantry door. It is full dark, though only five o'clock. The UK is a long way north and in winter the days are short, and we are now into late autumn. We follow a path I have plotted for us that avoids as many cameras as possible. Wet twigs and leaves brush my face and crunch underfoot. I try to keep us to the grass, but the lights from the house fall gold into the dark, making us throw shadows as we dash between them. Above all, I try to keep us from the gravelled path. Evie has the hem of my tee shirt gripped tight and sometimes her head bumps my back. We scuttle the final few metres and I ease the pantry door open. I press Evie against the outer wall and walk in and casually switch out the corridor light that leads to the kitchen. No one calls out to protest, so I wait a few moments. In the distance I can hear cat-calls as some of the men watch Saturday football.

I slide outside and grip Evie's arm guiding her through the darkness to the utility door, then gently push her inside. I shut her in and head out to check out the house. No one at all is in the screen room. The cameras are all transmitting pictures, but there is no one looking. Now is a good time. I hurry back, open the utility door and find Evie's forearm in the dark and grip it. She swings behind me, sheltering behind my bulk as we slip along the corridor past the door to the gym and into the kitchen, cross the brightly lit space, and enter another corridor, the one that leads to Hohne's study. Thankfully, it too is in darkness. At the study door, I edge it open, and check. There are two cameras in here that cover almost all of the room. I press my back hard against the wall and edge along to the first camera. Reaching up I mist Elnet over the lens. Evie tells me it is the best hair spray that there is with an extra fine spray. Certainly, the can is an expensive looking gold colour. I have taken her word for it, having no expertise in hair lacquer. Hopefully, this will smudge any images so even if we are seen, with the blurring and the darkness, we shouldn't be recognised. Sliding around the walls, I do the same to the second camera. Then I return to pull Evie inside.

As she steps hesitantly into the room, she pauses. I lean forward and nuzzling her neck I run the tip of my tongue down the sensitive skin that runs under her ear. She shudders, and I almost groan. She may be using me as a tool for her heist, but she is not completely indifferent to me. 'Hurry,' I whisper. I move to the window behind the desk and free the catches.

She doesn't mess about. Using the light on her camera she finds the computer and fires it up. Her fingers move like a wildfire in brush. I have never seen anyone type so fast. I step to the door and lean against it. I have told Evie, any trouble and she is to go out of the window. Whatever happens, I want her safe, and we couldn't be in any more danger right now. I daren't stand in the corridor for fear of someone wondering why I am lingering around.

My eyes are now fully used to the dark, and my ears are straining for footsteps in the hall. Evie is waiting now, her face lit by the glow of the computer and she has never looked more beautiful to me. She is focused, intent, using skills she has honed over years. She is the one with the vision, she is the one who is trying to change the world, and I am overwhelmed with admiration.

And my job is to keep her safe. And I fail. I don't hear footsteps, I don't hear speech, all that happens to tell me we have failed is the door pushing hard against my back. I spin to put all of my weight and strength into holding it in place. 'Go!' I hiss to Evie. I lean in harder, but my feet are being forced to slide across the carpet. 'Go,' I say again, but I do not hear the window moving. As I spin my head to try and see where she is and what she is doing, the door receives a massive shove and I am forced backwards. DuPaul, Manon and Dunbar step silently into the room, Dunbar throwing the lights. Evie is standing behind the desk, unmoving. Why didn't she run?

As I rush forward to go to her DuPaul and Manon grab at my arms and one is forced painfully up my back. I don't care, they can dislocate it if they want, I need to get to Evie. A blow to my back sends me to my knees and I feel the cold barrel of a gun pressed to my temple. When I still struggle, the gun is used to bash my head. Dazed, I try to see where Evie is. Dunbar, a wiry Irishman who has made it clear he hates me, has her in a choke hold. 'No,' I yell, but my voice comes out hoarse.

Then the cherry on the cake, Hohne walks in. I look up at him from my kneeling position on the ground, Manon still holding my arm high up my back, the gun still pressed to my temple.

'I left you at the club,' I say.

'Mm. I decided to leave. A friend brought me home in his Rolls. I really must get one. I always thought that they were rather passé, but I was quite impressed.'

He looks over to Evie. 'Ah, Ms Scott. How nice to be in your company again.'

I buck and strain and DuPaul gives me a neat clip on the head with the gun.

'Release Ms Scott, Dunbar, I am sure you can subdue her without breaking her neck. At least, not yet.'

Dunbar grins, he pulls one of Evie's hands behind her yanking it up her back, and with the other he grips her breast to hold her tight to his body. I shove against the floor with a roar and almost make it to my feet. DuPaul's wet mouth is on my ear. 'Settle down, or I will have to pull the trigger.' I stop, panting.

'Bring them to the gymnasium,' Hohne instructs.

For the first time I am afraid. Three men and Hohne I reckon I have a chance of taking. But not in the gym. Too many weapons for us all to grab. And it is underground. And sound will not carry from there. When I begin to struggle furiously Manon jerks my arm higher bringing my head down to the floor and DuPaul leans in to yell, 'Stop, fucking, struggling.'

Both Evie and I are put into plasticuffs. For the first time I catch her eye. Her eyes are blank, her face white. Did she not realise that this might happen? Suddenly she realises I am looking straight at her. Her face softens and she mouths something at me. It can't be what I think it is.

We are frogmarched down the hall and across the kitchen to the door that leads to the underground gym. We all, except Hohne, stumble down the stairs either being restrained or restraining. Hohne walks down as if he owns the world and is pausing in his busy life to regard the wild-life. Well, I suppose he does. Him and the other billionaires. Once in the gym I am forced to my knees again, this time my hand-cuffed hands being held high so I am forced to tip forward, my nose almost on my knees. Evie's name is flying around inside my head. How do I get her out of this?

'What were you two doing in my study?'

'Finding out how you make your money,' I say. Twisting I see that Evie has blood running down her chin from where Dunbar has hit her. Rage blinds me and I begin to fight again. Another bash on the head from the gun makes me pause. This hitting my head is getting old.

'Dunbar, leave the woman alone. You are far too good for her.'

The slur sends me swinging my head from side to side.

Hohne's smooth voice cuts through the pain. 'I thought I had you nicely tamed, Marco. Your poor, poor parents. To lose one son is a shame, to lose two a tragedy. Perhaps I will try and find the third one in Germany. Why not do the triple? I would have to put off the parents of course. I would need to know that they suffered. I don't want death to come as a relief.'

And then we all freeze in place. A noise we are all familiar with echoes upstairs. A shot. I know that here are only two men left in the house, either on duty or asleep upstairs, I am not sure which. I didn't take the time to find out, I just wanted Evie to do her stuff and get her out of there. For a moment we are all too stunned to move, then Hohne says,

'Shoot them.' He turns to walk towards the stairs pulling a gun out from his back waistband. Before he has fully turned around, there is a blinding noise that echoes off the mirrors and blank walls. DuPaul has lifted the muzzle of his gun and shot Hohne in the back of the head, while Manon has shot Dunbar. Evie has her mouth open and is probably screaming, but I cannot hear. DuPaul's gun was right beside my head. With swift movements DuPaul and Manon free us both. I meet DuPaul's eyes, and he winks. Then he takes a quick stride towards Evie and presses a credit card into her hand. His mouth is moving but I can't hear what he is saying, but Evie has taken the card and is nodding. There is blood and brains on her hair and right shoulder. I push to my feet and sweep a discarded towel into my hand. Blood is one thing but I don't want her to realise exactly what is coating her hair. I grab her hand and we follow DuPaul and Manon at a run.

At the top of the gym staircase Evie pulls on my hand. I am twisting to run to the other side of the house and escape, but she is off like a hare back towards the way we came. I curse; she is heading for the study. I chase after her. Dimly through the ringing in my ears I am aware of shots. As we cross the kitchen we crunch over broken window glass. The police will be here soon, and they will come with guns and dogs. Evie flies into the study just as I reach her, she grabs the computer and hauls it into her arms, then looks to me and gives me a nod, holding out one hand. I grab it and pull her back into the hall. Through the pantry door on my right we can see flashes of light, so I go back to plan A and head back through the kitchen.

As we reach the entrance to the kitchen some pottery storage jars up on a shelf explode. Thank heavens Carla is not on duty. Shots are now flying all around the huge open space. Clearly there is a gun-fight close outside and many bullets are going wide. We crouch down and using the kitchen units for cover we scramble across.

We are half-way to the opposite entrance when an oven door is hit and fine glass particles mist into the air. 'Don't breathe,' I yell, reaching behind me to pull Evie's sweatshirt hem up over her face. And then the air is full of wine bottles. One crashes above my head on the worksurface, one hits the units right in front of us. Molotov cocktails. Bottles of accelerant with flaming rags shoved into the bottle mouth. Only some of the rags have fallen out as the bottles fly through the air. I tut at the incompetence. An unlit bottle reaches the opposite units again, and where the last bottle bounced and smashed on the floor so the flames licked over the tiles spreading slowly, this one spills its contents down the front of the cabinet. Flames fly up the front of the unit from the floor, and the fancy designer paint on the doors catches alight. The kitchen is rapidly becoming an inferno.

I reach for Evie. She has her hands over her ears and is shaking uncontrollably. Not surprising. Someone wanted to shoot her in the head and now she is sitting in the middle of a bonfire. I pull her into me. She has a death grip on the computer and I have to prise one hand free so I can pick her up. I stand, with her clutched to my front, her face buried into my neck, and her hands behind my back, linked by the wretched laptop. I don't run to the way out. The floor is slippery with accelerant. When I reach the part of the floor that is alight, I steady Evie, and run, hoping my trainers don't catch alight as they splash through the liquid. As we reach the carpet in the hall, there is a whoosh sound and the kitchen really begins to burn.

I pelt down the hall holding Evie tight and into a fancy dining room beautifully laid out for a dozen people or more. I reach the window, haul it open and forcing Evie from my arms, throw her out. She lands in the flower border below and I launch myself after her. Rather than mess around, I run for the main gate, Evie's hand tight in mine. The intruders came at the house from the back, the police will arrive at the front, and I'd rather meet them than the lunatics with guns behind me.

I slam a hand against the button that opens the gates and they begin to grind their cumbersome weight open. We squeeze through the gap as soon as we reach it, not waiting for a bigger space. The heavy metal continues to move silently, well, at least to me, to its open position and we are off and running down the street, sliding into a back alley-way the moment we can. We duck and dive in and out of backways and main roads as we head back to Evie's, sometimes running other times fast-walking, panting and buzzing from adrenaline. Evie is coming out of her frozen state of shock and is doing well, keeping up. We say nothing.

As soon as the outer door to her apartment is closed I reach for Evie and begin to haul her clothes off her. 'Shower,' I instruct. 'Wait,' she mumbles through the sweatshirt I am pulling over her head. 'Shower,' I insist. I want all of that blood and gore off her, preferably before she has a close look. 'Wait,' this time a wail. She is now in her tracksuit bottoms and bra. She reaches in and fumbles twos credit card out of the bra. She is vibrating like a mis-firing engine the shock still controlling her. 'Take it,' she says, shoving one into my hand. I ignore her and begin to untie her trainers. 'Marco, book flights to Scotland on the next plane possible.' Her hand is shaking so hard the card drops to where I am working down at her feet pulling her shoes off. I pick up the card and read the name. 'Whose is this?' I ask.

'Yours, please, go and book the bloody flights.' Her voice is shaky and full of tears.

I pull her trackie bottoms off and then take her firmly by the arm and tug her into the bathroom. I start the shower without turning on the bathroom light, going just by the borrowed light falling in from the main room. Once it is lukewarm, I gently push her in.

'All you have done tonight is manhandle me,' she complains. That sounds better.

'Wash,' I say, and leave her in the dark, the water falling down onto the top of her head. Hopefully, by the time she steps out to put the light on, the worst of the results of tonight will be sluiced out of her hair at least.

I pick up the phone and book us on a flight to Scotland. We don't need passports for that and it gets us a few miles from London, which feels a good idea at present. I have to tell the woman making the booking that I am deaf, but can hear her if she speaks slowly and clearly. Bless her, she shouts the booking reference down the phone. Now I strip and bend to rummage under the sink for a large plastic waste bag. I put everything we were wearing in it, including my watch and our shoes. As Evie comes back into the room, still shaking but a bit less so, I take her place in the shower. When I step out she says, 'Wear these,' and throws a pair of jeans, a white tee shirt and a zipped jacket at me. Socks follow. Everything sort of fits. I find a box with black trainers under the jeans. They are tight but I can walk in them.

'I rang an Uber while you were showering. The flight isn't until the morning so I have booked us into an airport hotel for the night.'

Her phone tings, and she says, 'That must be the car.' We are both panting as if still running.

I take both bags. Evie grabs two backpacks and hands me one, and we hurry down the stairs to the car.

The hotel is a concrete box but does the job. The room is warm, which I am glad of as Evie is still shivering. Hardly removing her coat she immediately sits at Hohne's computer linking it to her own. I watch her for a moment as she hunches over the screens completely focused on what she is doing. The concentration has made her brain stop thinking about the events that have put her into shock. I pull out my phone and go to the BBC news. There is a bright red banner running along the bottom of the screen saying that gang warfare has broken out in central London. The presenters are reading excitedly from their auto-cues about a gun battle and a blaze at one of the most up-market addresses in London. There are helicopter or drone shots of Hohne's place on fire. It is well ablaze now and the whole area is golden with firelight. I see that the next-door neighbour has moved all of his limos out onto his drive. I would have thought they would have been safer in the garage. He won't be able to move them away as the whole area is blocked off with fire engines and police and ambulance vehicles. Along with the light from the fire that ebbs and swirls as the flames roar into the night sky, there is now the strobing of red and blue from the emergency vehicles. It is a scene from a disaster movie. I move to other news sites, but no one so far is putting up pictures or names of 'persons of interest'. I breathe a sigh of relief. As Evie sits back and rubs her back I say,

'We aren't famous yet.'

'Good, I don't ever want to be. A life in the shadows suits me just fine. And Hohne is now broke. I have moved every penny he ever squirrelled away and hidden from the tax authorities. And I have back dated the documents by a month and the Goldingtons now have eight billion pounds and a super yacht.'

'Do you trust them?'

She breathes in deep. 'Well, it will go one of two ways. They will keep the lot and have a great life and why not after decades of public service? I think they deserve it more than a people and drug smuggling evil nonentity like Hohne.' I snort at hearing Hohne called a nonentity. He loved the think he was a great man, it was in his every swagger. 'On the other hand, they have served for decades in public service. They have seen in their daily working lives just how much people need help, support, medical care and I think that they want to do good. They will get fleeced, bound to happen, they will mismanage, but at the end of the day I don't care. You don't give something and then worry about how it is used. It is a gift, not a set of handcuffs.'

I look at her sitting there. Evie. Hair everywhere in tangles, clothes cheap and just tossed on, and chain store trainers on her feet. And she is beautiful. 'Have I ever told you how impressed I am by you?'

Me?' she says.

'Yes, you.' I stand and take her hand. 'Are you all finished up here? Because if so, there is a bed there that needs some company.'

And she grins. And she pulls my head down for a long deep kiss. And all is right in my world. Prison may beckon for us both, but at the moment it is only beckoning.

. . .

While we wait to board the plane in the morning I search online and find us a cottage to rent for a month. It is remote and we will have to use the car for groceries, but it is cheap, and I still think like a working man who watches his pennies. The news is now hysterical about the gun battle. The fire is out, and what was my home for three years is now a pile of ash. I feel rather sorry for the cars. I kept them looking beautiful and perfectly maintained; it seems a shame that they can now be seen peeping as ashy metal through the roof tiles and rubble of the garage. The guy next door lost his as well. Moving them was not his best idea.

As we stand in the queue to board the plane a woman taps me on the shoulder. I try not to heave up. Being investigated by the police bothers me more than a little. I had a taste of that with Evie's ex; I really don't look forward to being interviewed again. I turn, to find an attractive woman probably in her late forties with curly hair looking up at me.

'I think I recognise you,' she says, and I feel Evie freeze next to me. 'Aren't you on the British Olympic team.'

Relief makes me dizzy. I smile down at her, holding her eyes. 'No,' I say, in my thickest Serbian accent, 'I am Serbian lorry driver.'

'Oh,' she says. I run my gaze deliberately up and down her body, pausing for a moment on her breasts. I lean to speak into her ear, 'We have many beautiful men in Serbia. You should go.' I stand and give her my wickedest smile, 'A woman like you would be much appreciated.'

We turn to move ahead in our queue and Evie shoots me a glance. 'Flirt,' she mutters. Her hair is piled primly up onto her head so I lean forward and run my tongue up her neck to her ear. I hear a gasp from the woman behind. Evie shoots me an evil look, then turns forward grinning.

In Edinburgh we hire a car on forged driving licences. 'Who is this guy who is doing all of this forgery for you?' I ask. Evie looks at me and pulls in her lips. I wonder if she will refuse to tell me, then she says, 'I found him on Hohne's computer.'

'So Goldington didn't know anyone.'

'No, as it turns out.'

'Can you trust the guy?'

She looks at me as if I am simple. 'Of course not.' And it seems that conversation is over.

The cottage is as promised. Down a long single-track length of tarmac with a fantastic view of the sea way below us. I vow to walk the hills and cliffs the cottage stands on as soon as I can, for as long as I want. It is beginning to dawn on me that my time is my own. I am free. I don't feel free, as yet, and watch the news obsessively. The forensic people are still sifting through the rubble of the house according to the news and the police have revealed little. The longer they delay putting out news, the more I worry. Evie and I didn't start the gun battle or burn the house down, but we have committed a huge fraud. Or is it robbery? I wonder what the difference is but decide it doesn't matter. We stole stuff. Even if it was from a bad guy. I am not sure what response standing in court and saying, 'We had to steal it your honour, he was a really nasty person,' might receive.

Because I am a known employee of Hohne, with face and finger-prints known to the police, Evie's plan is for me to change my appear-ance drastically and then leave the country, while she reckons as long as she has a passport in another name, she can alter her looks easily.

'I will have my hair cut short and bleached blonde and wear glasses. If I dress in heavy-tread boots and long flowing skirts, my own mother would never recognise me.' I blink. I am not certain even I would, and I have explored every millimetre of her skin. Thinking that makes me hot. Evie, ever the mind reader slaps my hand, 'Down boy,' she says. I laugh and hug her to me. Warm, wonderful, Evie. Who will discard me one day. But, if my luck holds, not today.

Evie is completely convinced that she can leave the country on a forged passport and an adjustment to her looks. 'I shall limp,' she says. 'I have read in crime novels that it is a good disguise to alter your gait.' I just stare at her. Ok, but I am almost two metres tall and almost as wide. I can't limp my way through customs.

'I am sorry,' she says. 'I could perm your hair and bleach it white. If you then wore reading glasses that we can pick up at any store I suppose you might away with it. And don't forget to limp. But I am not confident enough that that will work. I am not going to risk you being picked up by the authorities so I will disguise you thoroughly,' she says. 'But first I will have to wax you all over.'

Wait a minute, we haven't discussed this. 'What?' Hang on, that is masochistic female shit.

'You will be fine.' She leads me into the bathroom and sits me on the toilet seat. A ton of stuff is loaded into the dry wash-hand basin. I sit, frowning.

She begins on my legs and I yell and yank the leg out of the way. The second strip of wax is even more painful. She stands frowning at me, hands on hips.

'You are flinching before I have touched you. Either stop, or I will blindfold you.'

'I like the idea of blindfolds. Can I do you without the painful stuff?'

She looks even crosser. 'No.' And leaves the bathroom. When she returns she has a silk scarf in her hand and she ties it tight around my eyes. 'Now, let us get on.' Chastised, I man up and take it. It bloody hurts though.

Finally, she says that this is the first stage on of my transformation finished and we will do the next bit tomorrow to let my skin recover. I grip her backside and pull her close and huff warm breath onto her tummy. 'I demand reparations in pleasure for all that pain,' I say, and pulling her top up begin to nibble and lick and kiss her wonderful skin.

'Stop it,' she says, but she is laughing. We leave the floor covered in used wax strips. As I slide onto the bed tugging her by the hand the covers feel rough. 'I hurt!' I complain.

She climbs across me. I am in nothing but boxers. 'Poor baby, I will just have to do all the work and be gentle with you,' she says as she whips off her top. Oh yes!!!

The following day she insists she covers my eyes again. 'You are such a wimp, I don't want you wriggling and interfering.'

She begins to smooth some stuff over my neck and shoulders,

working it into the skin. Having her cool hands run over my body when I cannot see where they will touch next is a terrific turn on. Which, as I am in my boxers only, she is well aware of. Suddenly she pulls at the top of my boxers and her hot, blissful, mouth takes my erection in. I instantly reach for her head and groan. She swats my hands away, and begins to suck as she caresses my length. Taking away sight is not a kink I have tried. I am now a convert.

Eventually, we cool down and return to the business in hand. My grin is a permanent fixture on my face.

Her hands slide across the skin on my legs. 'Are you putting make-up on me?'

'Have you ever heard of Vitiligo?' she asks.

'No.'

'It is a condition where the pigmentation of the skin goes random. Whatever colour your skin is, it can affect you. There have been cases of black people going completely white. White skins tend to have brownish-pink splotches. The people with it feel highly visible and are often made to feel uncomfortable.'

'So what are you rubbing into me?' I reach up to pull off my blindfold. She smacks my hand away.

'It is a skin dye. I researched the condition and there are some products only recently being produced that can cover the problem semi-permanently. If people want to. Some completely embrace their look and say it is a problem for other people if it bothers them.'

Her hands are sliding over my back now. 'So, exactly what are you doing to me?'

'Turning you black. You are European in colouring. Even with a dark tan you would be identified as white. People look at you. Women want you and men want to be you.'

Can't say that hurts my ego. But I am frowning. 'Are you going to do all of me?' I ask.

She bites her lip. 'What do you think? We obviously need to do your face, neck and hands but I think I should do some other areas that might show. If I hadn't done your legs, you would have to wear long trousers all the time.'

'Ok, I guess, I'd like to be able to wear shorts.' Especially as we are heading to Los Angeles.

'I bought a whole-body size pack, only I am not sure it is your body size, so you will have a white band around your middle until I can see how far this stuff goes.'

'And will you still want me when I am black?' I haven't got my head around this yet.

She nuzzles the side of my neck. 'Marco, I would want you if you we green or fluorescent orange or blue. Your colour would never matter to me.'

Want me, not love me. I hear her loud and clear.

Chapter Nine

I stare into the mirror above the wash-hand basin. Then I walk to the long mirror Evie uses that is fixed to the back of the wardrobe door. I am a black man. I feel sick. I stare, then flex my hands in front of my face. They are not mine. Clearly my horror has been picked up by Evie. The cream was a pale lemon colour when Evie stroked it on, but it has developed rapidly and now I can see my face, the last area she did, going darker and darker.

'Marco?' she says softly.

'This,' I don't have the words, 'this is an abomination.'

'What do you mean?' she whispers the words.

'I can't go into public looking like this. It is every shape of wrong.'

'You have to. No one will be looking for a black man, how else can I get you out of the country? You are far too physically distinctive for simply a new name on a passport. We discussed this.'

'No,' I say, 'no we didn't. And even if we did, I had no idea I would feel like this.'

She swallows audibly and says, 'What is so wrong, Marco?'

'I am posing as something I am not, and never can be.'

'What if you wore an electrician's overall and carried a tool box? That would be a disguise.'

'But being black is more than skin colour. It is about the legacy of slavery and exploitation. Even a dumb ox like me knows that.'

She drops her head, then gathers her strength and stares at me. 'What you are talking about is cultural appropriation.'

'I have no idea. I just know how bloody, bloody uncomfortable it feels.'

Her eyes are full of tears now and her voice angry. 'Well, just suck it up. I am going into town for groceries.'

I hear her rummage around for a few minutes, and then the outer door slams and the car fires up. I stare a bit longer into the mirror, then go to find a pair of track-suit bottoms and a long-sleeved top. With gloves and a ball cap I should be fairly invisible if I keep away from the regular paths. I need to move. To run out this sense of guilt and discomfort. I didn't see this coming. Not any of it. And if she had told me beforehand, I would have agreed to it, I would never have considered how guilty I might feel. But she is right. I look beyond different. It should work; this gives me a real chance to leave the country. I leave the cottage open as I have no idea if Evie has a key and run up the nearest hill. And I keep running. As I run I realise that Evie's Christmas present was stashed in my wardrobe at Hohne's place. Christmas is only days away now, and I will have nothing to give her. I run harder. Trying to escape myself.

Evie comes back and begins cooking. Steak, oven chips, and red wine. With a salad so we don't feel too guilty. We are good again, just a little strained. I realise that my hearing is much improved. Give it a few days and it should be back to normal. Google tells me it is all about little hairs. A loud noise flattens them like a strong wind over grass. If the noise is far too loud, then the hairs never stand up again and the result is deafness. I send a mental memo to my tiny flattened hairs to say that they would be far happier standing tall like little soldiers.

Across the table as we dig into some excellent local steak, Evie asks, 'What are you thinking so intently about?'

'Erections,' I say.

'Men,' she mutters and buries her head in her dinner once more. And I grin. And blow her a kiss.

The news that night is not good for us. The police have worked out that no women were in the fire and have identified Evie as a 'person of interest'. I suspect the fact that she immediately disappeared has given them that idea, along with the fact that they know that we know each other. A couple of Hohne's men have been identified, but forensics are still working on four other male bodies. And then my, DuPaul, and Manon's pictures flash up. The police are 'concerned' about Evie, us, they just want to get their hands on. We hold each other tight in the night.

We take new photos and send them off to Evie's forger. They come back by return of post. Clearly the man had everything prepared except for the pictures. We can now head for the airport and flights to Los Angeles. Hanging around the airport is hell. We are both on edge. Every minute crawls by. When we are delayed for fifteen minutes Evie squeezes my hand so hard the blood stops flowing. Once in the air, she lets out a huge sigh. 'They might still be waiting at the other end,' I say 'it is an eleven-hour flight.' 'Cassandra,' she mutters, and I grin. She turns and stares out of the window, but she never lets go of my hand. Cassandra was cursed to prophecy the truth but never to be believed. I hope I am not a Cassandra; I don't want what I said to be the truth but the idea that we might have got away simply seems too improbable.

We say little, and I allow myself a couple of beers. I have plenty of time to sober up before we land. I might be Mr Control, but Evie is clearly Ms Efficiency. Evie knocks back gin like it is lemonade, until she slips into a restless doze. I wrap her in the duvet the airline supplies and ease a pillow under her head. Her hair is soft and silky under my hands and I let it slide through my fingers. This might be the last time we are together. As I see it, my usefulness has come to an end. I watch a film without seeing a frame and slide into a light sleep. Every moment I expect to be handcuffed and told we are to be arrested.

We arrive, blinking into the airport lights at Los Angeles and discuss whether to wait for our suitcases. On the grounds that they are under false names we won't be using for much longer and suitcases go missing all the time, we decide to leave them and get out into the heat and gridways of the city as quickly as possible. A taxi takes us to a huge downtown hotel and we book in with only our backpacks, explaining that our luggage has gone missing, which is kind of the truth. Once safely in the room and living under our second set of false names, we crawl into bed and fall into exhausted sleep. I have shoved a heavy side table against the door. It won't stop anyone who wants to get in, but hopefully it will slow them a little so we have time to wake. I decide that 'do not disturb' signs are the best invention ever, as sleep over-whelms me.

When I awake, Evie's back is curled into my front and my arm is wrapped around her waist. I breathe in, and then move her hair to one side and kiss the smooth skin below her ear.

'You have a thing about the side of my neck,' she murmurs.

'I have a thing about all of you,' I tell her.

She rolls to face me, slides a hand behind my head, and kisses me deeply. I don't need telling twice.

As it is still daylight we contact the plastic surgeon Evie has researched, and go to see him. He is shifty, and I am terrified. The idea of trusting him to give me anaesthetic and cut into me with knife makes me sick to my stomach. That night we argue about it, but deep inside I have to agree with Evie. We were both known to Hohne and we have vanished. To any police that is screaming guilty. Cameras all over the world can be programmed to look for us, and we want to be able to move around freely, not hide in some backwoods corner. And a shoot-out in one of the most expensive parts of London is big news. Huge. When we get back to our room and switch on the tv it comes up with CNN. A picture of Hohne's house in Onslow Square is on the screen along with news about the police investigation. The announcer seems more than happy that London has suffered a major gun crime.

'I wonder if DuPaul was involved in the fire, or if it was all Xaviera. Fire gets rid of DNA.' I am relieved that Xaviera has been identified as one of the dead. He is the kind of guy who might come after us just for the hell of it.

'That reminds me,' she says. She goes to her computer and starts her fingers flying about the keypad.

I frown and ask, 'What are you doing?'

'Putting a million pounds into DuPaul's bank account. Half for each. Fair do you think?'

'I have no idea,' I say. I watch her face, so focused. I guess half of a million pounds for each of us is reasonable. We wouldn't be alive but for him. And he probably doesn't really believe we would send him anything at all.

Surgery is booked for two days time. I burn the passports we used to escape the UK in the wash basin and flush the ashes, that stink, down the waste, hoping all the time that I don't set off the smoke alarms. They stay quiet. Clearly they are set that a burnt passport is fine while tobacco is not. I go back to arguing about whether we can trust the surgeon and the air between us becomes fractious. We are both on edge. Evie spends hours on her computer while I go shopping for something comfortable to wear, hiking gear, and work out in the gym. But every night she holds me close and we make love. I wonder if it is for comfort, like a child with a soft rag. I make the most of it. Every touch is precious, every kiss a memory. To hold her in my arms makes me complete and I would hold her forever if she would let me.

The surgery goes well and when we return to the hotel puffy and bruised after two days in a private recouperation centre we receive many knowing looks. Evie is clever. Los Angeles is the plastic surgery centre of the US, as so many wannabe actors come here and then decide they need a new nose, or a bit of a lift. One older receptionist tells me in a low voice, 'Honey, I would have ripped those pants off you just the way you were. Why go and spoil your pretty looks?' I blow her a kiss and the comment cheers my day. We need to rest for a couple of weeks and decide to rent a villa with a pool beside the coast in Mexico. I have never been to either the US or Mexico before. As soon as we are over the border the food improves.

'We have been eating in the wrong restaurants. There must be Mexican places in the US.'

Evie gives me a sour look and continues to eat her taco as if she hasn't eaten for a week. We have been keeping low key. Perhaps too low key. Then she smiles at me and the sun comes out. Surely now we are rich, we can eat a bit more upmarket? I decide not to push it. But I am a big guy. I need my carbs.

The winter we left behind in the UK was grim, and for two weeks with great delight we lay in the sun. We need to keep our faces protected, but we can paddle in the ocean, eat our heads off, and I even learn to drink tequila. Only a couple though. Ever since I met Hohne I am terrified of someone coming up and shoving a knife or putting a bullet into me. I wonder if I will every feel relaxed enough to believe I don't need to be permanently vigilant. As my face heals I learn my new looks. My nose is great. It was busted during a fire fight in Chechnya, and basically I shoved it back into place and carried on. My very square chin has had its corners softened and he has done something to my ears. Such small changes, yet it unsettles me. Evie is able to go straight to our end destination with a final new passport, but I need to hide away until the colour has left my skin. And that I cannot wait to happen. I do not have imposter syndrome. I am an imposter.

'What are you thinking?' she asks one morning.

'That it was a crime to put someone as beautiful as you under the knife, and I can't see any difference. You are just as lovely as you were.'

'My eyes lift a little at the edges.'

I shake my head. 'I don't see it, and I am glad. I liked you just the way you are. When you wear makeup I just want to lick it off. You are perfect, you don't need it.'

Her blush is deeper now. 'Lick it off,' she murmurs, and my mind goes dirty.

We live quietly while we heal. Evie reads about a book a day while I run and hike anyplace I can. In the afternoons when I have showered and napped I like to rip her bikini off with my teeth. It is my favourite new thing. She usually shoves me into the pool, but I can generally man-handle her in after me. I especially enjoy it when she runs naked and screaming through the house as catching her lights my fire. Apart from her nightmares about shots and flames, life is good.

When the bruising is almost invisible, we take photos and Evie applies for a new UK passport. She has all the false documentation necessary. This one will not be a forgery, well it is really, but this one will be legitimately made by His Majesty's Government itself. Her new look, name and ID will all be settled. Ms Evalinda Hope will replace Ms Eve Scott on this Earth, with a birth certificate and insurance number and all the rest to prove it. She is to head immediately to the Caribbean.

I need time to become white again and to also apply for a passport with my new face. The plan is that when I have similar forged documents as Evie, I will join her in the Caribbean. Meanwhile, I apply for a Long Distance Permit for the Pacific Crest Trail, along with a California Fire Permit. The PCT is a walking trail that runs for over 4,000 kilometres pretty much from Mexico to Canada along the US west coast. I like the idea of a hike and being out in the wilds and only dependent upon myself. I have been imprisoned by my life for too long; I want to feel free. I am sick of wondering if there is a bullet or knife around every corner, and if anyone wants to come and find me on the Trail, whether Interpol or some gangland killer, then good luck to them.

We part the day Evie's new passport arrives. I drive her to the airport and sit like the fool I am until I see her flight rise into the air. Even then I watch until it is beyond doubt that it is out of my sight. There are bears on the trail I am to take. If one rips out my guts with its claws I couldn't feel more pain. I have serious doubts that when, or if, I land in Barbados Evie will be there. Deep inside I believe that we are over, despite what I think I saw her mouth at me when we were captured in Hohne's office. After all, we thought we were going to die and she hasn't said it since. I return the car, and take a bus to a town where I can later walk to pick up the Pacific Crest Trail.

The PCT is tough. I start in desert, but will eventually climb up into the snow-line of mountains. I am hoping to get far enough to see, and touch, the giant redwoods that I have read about. The idea of laying a hand on a living being that is over 1000 years old thrills me. Camping out at night is necessary, as although there are way-stations, they are few and far between. The hike was my idea. I am used to looking after myself in tough conditions. It will be a little like being back as a soldier, though without the friendship that made it bearable. However, my experience of hikers is that they are a convivial bunch and I am sure I will have company now and then. The challenges will take my mind off the ache of missing Evie and I will meet different people every day so no one will be aware of my fading colour. The best bit is, no mirrors, so I don't have to catch sight of myself reflected anywhere. I set out feeling stoic. What will be will be. And after years of feeling trapped, I can revel in the freedom of being self-reliant.

I set off at dawn on day 1, only to finally reach the actual trail to find that I am far from alone. Glancing around I realise that there must be at least thirty others either setting off or hiking through. This is not what I expected. I pull my ball cap down lower and join the throng. This is not the absolute beginning of the trail but it is, I suppose, fairly close. I hate being black in public. I thought I would look like a 'blacked-up' white, but am surprised how natural it looks. Tata has a mate back home, they work in the same factory together, who is from Senegal, and I could pass for his brother or cousin. The idea makes me more, not less uncomfortable. The screaming sense of being an imposter prevents any rational thought, all I can concentrate on is keeping my face hidden and as far from everyone else as possible.

By the end of a hot day the clump of walkers has thinned out, and are now strung along the trail. My stride becomes more lose, and finally, as night drifts in, I feel myself relax. I walk on by moonlight for a while, before settling to camp. I roll into my sleeping bag after scarfing a pack of dry rations, but sleep does not come easily. I want to think. I want to go over my life so far, face all my mistakes, and come to terms with my present. And then, I need to consider my future. Is what I feel for Evie that deep connection that could last a life-time? Or will being away from her make her insubstantial, someone who will always be a good, if rather sad, memory? What is real, and what is the result of extraordinary circumstances? I crave the space to think. And then my brothers. Miloje and Rodavan. For years I have tried not to let their names enter my mind. I think of them only as 'older brother' and 'younger brother'. I have never let the words that are their names pass my lips. Miloje is lost somewhere in Germany, and I miss him. Perhaps now I can go and find him; hunt him down. And Rodavan, the genius with a spanner who loved motor bikes both riding them and taking them apart. His name means 'happy spirit', and never was a boy better named. His face was full of smiles and grins and mischief from daybreak to when he finally fell asleep. He was born during my first spell in the UK. I returned home to a chuckling toddler whom I instantly adored.

And then there are my army comrades. The ones who joined up with me and did not come home when I did. I want to spend time on the trail giving each of them a day and saying a proper farewell to them. While I remember them, they live on. While anyone remembers them, they live on. I need to honour that. I had come home at eighteen to find Miloje a man. Smoking and drinking and working. Fully adult. And there was I, speaking my native language, according to him, with an English accent. He sneered at me, called me soft and un-Serbian. A traitor to my birth-right. After a few nights of trying to go out drinking with him and his mates, and being insulted and mocked, I joined the army. Every soldier has promised to give their lives in the service of their country. I couldn't see how more Serbian I could prove myself to be. It was only when I saw the bone-white shock on his face when I came home to tell everyone what I had done, that I saw his regret. I don't want to be the reason he has cut himself off from his family; I came back, relatively unscathed. I too was old enough to choose my own path. And I wanted to feel properly Serbian again. Being sent away had been my parent's choice; they wanted a better life for me than sweating over a factory bench. They did what they thought was right, but that is something I need to consider. It cut me off from my family and my friends; when I returned I was an outsider, it wasn't only Miloje who made me feel that.

The army was harsh. The Russian tanks had a lever for steering, not a wheel, and the drivers, like me, were often trapped inside if the enemy managed a direct strike. None of us had pride in what we did, and we did and saw terrible things. Eight years of driving my immaculate truck didn't get rid of the nightmares. But Evie did. Sleeping beside her, driving my body into hers, the nightmares did not stand a chance. It has been an interesting life. And now I need to make sense of it. And having decided that, sleep knocks me unconscious.

The distance I cover each day begins to increase without my trying. The way-stations are indeed full of people who are fun to be with, and I can often have a bed for the night, indoors and with a mattress, though as I move further north, the attraction wears off as I adjust once more to sleeping on the ground. A decent hot meal is never refused, though. I do get tired of the dried rations I am packing, though twice I manage to catch a fish with a simple line and hook. They are cooked over wood fires and as I eat I wish I could share the taste with Evie.

We agreed to have little contact for safety's sake. We are trying to completely disappear and reinvent ourselves so leaving traces all over the Web seems foolish. Also, I have little internet connection on the trail. And then, after two weeks, I reach a way-station, log in on their computer, and there is a message.

'500 million kisses in Nevada. I miss you.'

My heart flies. Not at the kisses, that means I am now a bona fide millionaire with an account hidden in the state of Nevada. No, it is the 'I miss you' that has my heart galloping and my hopes flying. She didn't need to say that. Then the doubts hit, but did she mean it? Why write it if she didn't? Evie isn't cruel. On the same day I look into a mirror for the first time in two weeks. I am still black, but my skin is definitely lighter than it was. I decide to be positive, about Evie and about the fading. Being a millionaire does not alter my mood one iota. Without a doubt, money makes life easier, but it cannot replace love or health.

The terrain alters, mostly gently, desert merging into brush, merging into trees, but sometimes in one day I move from warm greenery to a land of rock and snow. I spend one of those nights high on a ledge above the tree line with star and moonlight glancing off the snow making it glisten into something other-worldly. I shall remember than night forever, it was peaceful and utterly magical. I am revelling in the independence, of being completely responsible for my own safety, nutrition and kit. I rise when I wish, and sleep when I wish. Wash and eat when I wish. I am free in a way few people ever are and, I am surrounded by nature, the birds and creatures that scuttle in the night, the wind and sun, the huge pine trees that cloak this coast. My hair is past my shoulders and I have a beard. And joy in my heart. It is only when I am on my third pair of boots that I begin to think about stopping. Most hikers are limited by money. They cannot stay away from earning a living and they have little in savings. But that is not a problem for me. I could walk forever. But Evie is never far from my thoughts. I miss her, with an ache that is not easing.

In the end I walk for far longer and far further than I intended. I have been white for a while now, back in my normal skin. The truth is, I am a coward. Yes, I am enjoying the self-sufficiency and the way that I feel fitter than I ever did using gyms and running city pavements, but if I stop and fly to Barbados, will Evie be there to meet me? My new passport was waiting for me two way-stations back. I look at the photo, at my altered chin and nose, and am amazed at how different and yet how the same I look. As I scarf down a decent hot meal at a way-station, I decide it is time to face my fears. I ask around about the nearest public transport. There is a bus station 30 klicks away. My target is set.

Once I decide to go, it takes a matter of hours. I give my pack away to a Goodwill store, and any other kit that I believe might be useful. Board a Greyhound bus to a city airport, buy a couple of tickets, and I am high in the air, heading for heavens knows what. I sleep, eat, drink a little, and watch the clouds, my mind oddly empty. I arrive in Barbados in brilliant sunshine and walk through customs into the airport. As I blink in the brilliance of the light after the dim customs hall, a small figure in a white sundress drops what she is holding and runs full pelt across the floor. I shrug off my backpack and as Evie launches herself at me, I set one hand on her arse and one on the back of her head. Her mouth is fixed on mine and neither of us want to let go. When I can think I grip her hair and pull her head back. I yank, deliberately, and watch her blink. 'Tell me now, is this real? Because if it isn't, I am on the next plane out of here. Either you are mine, and mean it, or you aren't.'

'Yours,' she hisses, and shoves herself higher in my arms to plaster herself once more against my mouth. I should have come home earlier. Because, clearly I have a home.

Part Two

Chapter Ten

I dig my toes into the warm soft sand. I cannot yet see Marco, and I worry, just a little. And then, there he is, two arms, rising black against the sea in the morning light, stroking strongly towards me. Every morning he walks naked down the beach and swims out as far as he can. The local men who fish these waters tell me that they will see him swim out, past their boats, and then he lifts from the water and dives down and they know that the next time they see him he will have turned and be heading back to the shore. To me. A couple of the most superstitious whisper that either he is half dolphin or a sea god. As long as that means that they revere him, I don't mind.

When he is close enough he stands and tugs his hair free of its ponytail. His dark hair shines in the light, and falls below his shoulders. He has facial hair now, too. Not the bushy wild beard I expected, but a neatly trimmed point off his chin. He hated the plastic surgery. His strong square jaw was rounded slightly and, and this was the most effective in terms of facial recognition, his ears were moved slightly backwards. He stared in the mirror afterwards and I could feel his dismay. I suspect because, unwittingly, the surgeon had given him his younger brother's slightly softer features. What he did rather like, was that a large bump on the bridge of his nose from some earlier incident, was smoothed out. I have caught him stroking the new slope and smiling occasionally.

He waves, and I wave back. It is a rare morning that I am not here waiting for him. His skin is now a dark bronze and he is close enough now that I can see the water running over his shoulders, across his chest, and chasing into rivulets as they find a course through his abs. There is a moment when the rising sun catches at the water and he is studded with diamonds, and then he takes another step and the effect is lost. Two local boys in tee shirts and shorts have waded out to speak to him. He dips his head and listens intently. I smile inwardly. There is a small curl of skin and flesh nestling against his balls. It looks so insignificant and yet it can be so huge when he is hammering into me. Plunge it into cold water and it retreats to nothing. It is, to me, one of nature's marvels.

We have been here seven years tomorrow, and it will be Marco's birthday. A local metalsmith has made me a two-metre trident and it is to be his present from me. The guy laughed his head off when I put the order in. Parts of Barbados, including the part we live in, appear to me to be something like Britain might have been like in the 1950s. The older people are law-abiding and attend church on Sundays. They gossip and moan about each other but when someone is in trouble, there is nothing they won't give or do to help. On his part, Marco says it reminds him of the community he grew up in; close knit and supportive. Some of the younger ones are going off the rails a bit. They smoke weed and can't see why they should work hard for pitiful wages when they can steal from the tourists and fence the stuff easily. They lie and wriggle and everyone worries about them.

None of this was visible when we arrived. Marco did what Marco does, he sorted himself out a set of weights and fashioned a bench press out of waste wood he scavenged, and then after his morning swim he would pull on a pair of shorts and work out here on the beach. In the evenings, when the sun is beginning to take the sting of heat out of the day, he does yoga and Pilates. I do that with him and we vie with each other over who is the most flexible.

Over time, boys would appear peeking through the shrubbery, or idling in the water pretending not to watch. Eventually, they began to join in. From Marco simply doing his own thing, he is now a respected teacher. The local Police Chief came down at one point. I made him coffee and sat with him as we watched Marco handle the lads. Marco was strict. Anyone who worked out with him has to appear at least three times a week, many come every day. Weightlifting, he tells them sternly, is not something you pick up and put down. He doesn't see the irony, and I have never enlightened him.

I could see the Police Chief's point. Here was a strange white guy attracting young lads into his company. He has become 'Reggie' to us and a firm friend. When he has a lad heading for serious trouble, he tries to send them to Marco. 'Go see the white guy,' he tells them, 'become a real man.' I am not sure about his approach, but it has worked sometimes. We now have alumni, who bring their wives and babies to see us. That is beyond wonderful.

Marco thought I would want an air-conditioned palace, but by the time he arrived here I had bought a piece of land on the edge of the Platinum Coast. Our plot cost the same as a large apartment would in Central London or Manhattan. Barbados has little coast and people, like the lady, Dusty, who I bought from, simply do not sell. As she said, what do I need money for? I live in paradise and it costs me nothing. I eat the vegetables and fruits I grow and I am too old to uproot myself. I simply upped the price until she was dizzy with noughts.

I befriended her by accident. She fell over right in front of me and I helped her up and then escorted her home as I was so worried about her. We sat and drank tea, and then I pottered around her kitchen while she watched and told me about her life in Barbados, her childhood, her dead husband, her children. I washed the dishes and cleaned the sink. Then, only because I was so caught up in her tales, I kept pottering, wiping here, tidying there, and she kept talking. Well, I was caught up, but I had no intention of not owning her bit of paradise.

Her wooden home on the land was falling to pieces. By the time Marco arrived I had indeed bought her property, knocked down and rebuilt her home exactly as it had been except it was no longer rotten, and begun to build a similar small home deeper into her plot. I have signed a deed promising that I will not sell the land in my lifetime. As dead hands controlling the living that are left go, it falls on me lightly. This is my home, and I am not going anywhere. We have a bedroom, an open kitchen and living room, and a study for me. A veranda runs all the way around so that we always have shade and, just like my ancient friend, we grow vegetables and fruit. Huge palm trees surround us and we can walk across out of our own garden and onto our beach and the sea. She tells me she likes to hear me scream my pleasure in the dark of the night as it reminds her of when she was young. I have to say, when she said that, my blush was brick red, but somehow it was said with such acceptance, I stopped being embarrassed. Love and loving are the best parts of life, and she has taught me to be relaxed about that. The Victorians are long gone, and good riddance.

Marco's passport is Irish, he had an (allegedly) Polish father and Irish mother and his name is Michael Donnelly. I insisted on the Michael, his is my beloved Marco and I refuse to call him anything else. Me, I am Evalinda Hope. I have never had to explain to anyone who I am or where I came from, and I love that about this place. The fact that we absconded with a billion of pounds, but that we live so simply, is our major camouflage in our new lives. Billionaires like to flaunt their money and power, with huge yachts and massive environment-damaging cars. The room next to our bedroom is my study where I manage our finances. The fact about rich people is that money begets money. The easiest way to become ever richer is to begin being rich in the first place. Everyone here heats their water from a water-holding contraption on their roofs as solar panels have never worked in this climate. We have been privately and secretly funding research into how to make them work here, and four years ago our boffins cracked it. We now have a huge business that supplies most of the Caribbean and pays a ton of tax to the Barbados government that has allowed them to begin building a new hospital. I am currently researching how to provide a complete cancer centre to supplement what the government is able to do. People from all over the Caribbean will be able to use it.

Marco always denigrates himself. 'I am just a lorry driver,' he will say. What he cannot see is that he is the HR director of a profitable and growing international company. When I tried to explain that to him, he laughed and said that he had no idea what human resources meant and he had never sacked anyone. I can find and entice the scientists and engineers I need to make my dreams a reality, but keeping them? Probably not. I read about their work until I know almost as much as they do, I bribe with a huge salary and a flexible contract so no important part of their lives is compromised, and yes, they begin work. But it is Marco who keeps them with us. He listens to any gripes or concerns, especially about my abrasiveness, and smooths everything out. So far, we have only had one technician leave us and I suspect that woman will never be happy anywhere. Everyone on the payroll knows the Marco is the power behind my throne. I direct operations, am the public face, but he is the oil that keeps it all functioning. And it works. We complement each other perfectly in this way.

One of the best aspects of coming here was Marco's parents. They came, hesitantly at first, to stay on the island. They accepted the fact that they had to come via a circuitous route and have false passports and names completely in their stride. I suspect that they had understood more about Marco's situation than he realised. There is nothing like having a son shot through the head on your doorstep to make you wary or to bring home to you the dangers of crime.

We took them to our local bar and by the second night Marco's dad was sitting with three Barbadian men vociferously arguing politics. We sank our heads in our hands as the table was thumped and voices were raised. As we walked them back to their rented bungalow, to our amazement he couldn't praise his companions enough. Their visits became longer and longer and eventually we bought them a modern bungalow two streets back from our beachfront home. Mama loves it. I have caught her opening the fridge for no reason except to marvel at its size and chill. She has joined a local quilting group and her growing English is now spoken with a Barbadian accent. The fact that they are both devout Catholic helps; it gives them a community who want to accept them. If Tata could just keep it down a bit in the local bar life would be perfect.

I tracked down Marco's elder brother in Germany. I made the Web dance until I found him. His marriage had broken up and he had spiralled into drink and drugs. At first he would have nothing to do with us and then he was given a three-year prison sentence for possession and intent to supply. He has clearly been deeply shocked and ashamed by the sentence and we are all now in contact with him and when he is released we are hoping that he will come to Barbados. Gradually, we are drawing our family around us.

What the Goldingtons are doing with all the money we entrusted them with, we have no real idea and are not interested. They are now known philanthropists, famous for using their huge 'lottery' win for good causes. Us, we have enough life here to keep us busy. Marco has just turned to find me; his dozen or so lads are heading for the sea to cool off. It is full daylight now, and I suspect, from that look, he doesn't think I should only scream at night. I grin back at him as he comes over to find me. He has a huge, 'Evie' tattooed over his old military tattoo. When I asked him why, he said,

'To tell the world I belong to you.'

When I was alone, I wept over those words. I haven't often told Marco the truth. I did work for a private bank, but no banker could access what I claimed to be able to do. No, it was all by hacking the bank and Hohne's accounts. I hadn't lied when I told him about my research and my doctorate. The web is as bright as day to me, I roam around it at will.

When I met Lucas, I was giddy with joy as I had not so long had my eye surgery. After a life of living with huge thick lenses that enlarged my eyes it meant that I could finally see without glasses. I had felt ugly for most of my life, and was known as a geek, so friends were few and far between. My whole life up to then I had felt like an outsider. He knew I worked for the bank, but lack of confidence always had me dressing in dull clothes, the sort of thing a clerk might wear. And although Marco calls me 'his little Evie', I am little only to someone of his size. Dad was a tall, raw-boned Yorkshire man, and I take after him. I am, to be polite, study. Yes, I have quite large breasts that Marco adores, but I also have no waist and a large and solid backside. Dainty I am not.

So there I was, feeling physically unattractive, sexually innocent, and boringly dressed. I didn't look at all like the high-flying banker I was. Now, I can see that my insecurities were exactly what attracted Lucas to me; he feasted on female vulnerability. Pity for him, he didn't bother to look below the surface. Me, I was bowled over. Someone fancied me. Someone good-looking, smart and with a decent job. What was there not to like? He proposed quickly and I agreed so my mum could attend. I am not sure she understood what was happening, she was going downhill fast and actually died two years before I met Marco. But she had spent my childhood dreaming about my wedding day, and how she would ensure that I had the most wonderful dress money could buy. I was desperate to give her that day, and the dress was very pretty.

I never allowed Lucas to see my pay slip. He took access of my bank account and I let him, but what he saw was a fraction of what I was actually earning. I simply paid an amount I thought would bolster his ego in each month from my real account and let him believe I was subservient. But I was watching him, and wising up. If he had known that I was already earning five times what he was, he would have run a mile. As to telling him about my annual bonus, no chance.

When I had told Lucas I was leaving he had been incandescent. His little creature had dumped him. It was only then that I saw all of the real man. How manipulative and vicious he could be. He yelled at me, 'You can't leave me! I own you.' And he did hit me. Hard. And then kicked me to pieces. Marco and I have not so far had children, and I do wonder if it is because of that kicking? After my stay in hospital, he told them I had fallen down stairs, I was ever so 'good' for the next few months, meanwhile quietly seeing a lawyer and building my new identity. I had to find a new job, but thankfully that did not prove to be a problem. My new employers seemed quite relaxed about me having changed my name and oddly, I should have realised, didn't ask too many questions. My reputation and references were glowing and they had already noticed me as a rising star in the banking world. If a new name was what I wanted, then new name was what I would get. So, Hohne met me as Evie Scott, my married name completely wiped out.

Nearly every client the new bank dealt with was a billionaire, often multiple times over, and I began to be irritated. Mum and dad had been decent people, hardworking and law abiding. Most of these men, and our clients were all men, had either made their money by manipulating politicians or destroying people for money. The political types never stinted on pushing vast sums onto political parties and were constantly guilty of corrupt stock dealing as those same politicians had the inside goods on a great deal that the markets would have to do in the future. The more obviously crooked ones were involved in human trafficking, drug and arms running and the like. I saw the political manipulators as the same as the rest, but their games impoverished ordinary people like my mum and dad. It was always the rich who benefited.

And what did they do with their billions? Waste it on toys mostly. Cars, planes, boats, space ships. While the world was going to hell in a hand-cart with climate warming and wars everywhere I looked. So I decided to do something about it.

Marco always describes Hohne as a toad but he was actually a real silver fox. With his thick dark hair that was silvered at the sides, I found him attractive. He was of medium height and yes, he was a bit soft around the middle, but not many billionaires are as good looking. He had good teeth and smelt of a delicious cologne. And after Lucas had introduced me to dull as ditch water sex, I was ready to explore. I did mange some of his accounts and that was how we came into contact. The first time we met he walked in as I was bending away from him over a computer screen. I stood fully upright and turned, and caught a predatory look on his face. I kept my face blank, but held his eyes. His expression shifted to amusement, and that was when I wondered if he might be the one. There was only one dinner, and the senior board members did leave me alone with Hohne. Their conscious callousness made me angry, and fuelled my decision. That night I refused to be cowed and simply left, calling an Uber to take me home. The next morning no one said a word.

After that, Hohne's eyes, and an occasional drifting hand, let me know he remained interested. I remained as cool as ice, but always looked him straight in the eye. I knew I had him confused, and that bolstered my confidence. He wanted me, but wasn't sure if I was responding or not. I wanted to explore what sex with an interesting older man might teach me. If I had had just a little more experience I might have worried more about what I was letting myself for. All the modern romance books I had read revelled in women exploring their sexuality. I thought it was my turn.

I let this strange enticement go on for a while and then, as I was walking him to the door of my office one day I set my lure. He was expecting me to reach for the door handle but instead I leant my weight back against the panelling. With one fingernail I ran a sharp line down his cheek. He froze, his eyes flaring, and I knew then that I had him.

I said, 'A room at Claridges, Sundays only, no more no less,' and waited. Claridges is top dollar, Princes, sheiks, film stars, it is where they stay if they can afford it. He narrowed his eyes and then said,

'Agreed. Starting this Sunday. I will let you know the room number.' And then he left.

So when I was telling Marco I was visiting my poor old mum, I was actually seducing, and being seduced by, Hohne. In a luxury suite in an impressive top London hotel. Complete with sitting room, bathroom, study and, of course, bedroom. It was fabulous. I didn't know such high-quality bedding existed, the sheets were blissfully smooth. Nor toilets that would wash you and then air-blow you dry! Actually, I didn't like that much. It didn't feel safe.

I arrived with two crystal glasses and a seriously cheap bottle of

Spanish Carva from my local convenience store. Hohne blinked as I took everything out of my bag and set them on a small table.

'What on earth are you doing?' he asked, 'I will send for real champagne.'

'Try this,' I said, 'I prefer it.' To say I had knocked him off balance was to say the least. I requested that he find some background music, the quiet was banging on my ears, and when he had done that I shoved him in the chest and made him sit in a chair facing the bed. His eyes narrowed, but he went along with it. I began to remove my dull clothing. Underneath I was wearing a bustier with suspenders that were holding up sheer black stockings. And of course, I was wearing high, high heels. Manolo Blahniks, actually. I could easily afford them and they were surprisingly comfortable. When I saw Hohne shift in his seat, I stared pointedly at his groin. I was not wearing knickers, so I began to touch myself. His face began to go red, so I continued while he sat as still as a statue. I wanted to get myself started first as Lucas never bothered and I was fed up with feeling frustrated. I wanted to be thoroughly fucked for once.

Hohne didn't watch for long. And he was an excellent lover. That afternoon he rammed into me and shot all my frustrations into smithereens. And then he aroused me again and repeated the trick. And then did it again. I was well content. I now knew a number of positions beside missionary and a great deal more about what turned me, and him, on. After he had gone, I soaked my aches and pains away in the bath while watching the news on the large wall tv, sipping the champagne the hotel provided, nibbling utterly delicious canapes, and congratulating myself. I now had a lover. The next thing would be to decide what to do with him. It wasn't until our sixth meeting that the real man appeared. I was up, dressed and out of there in a flash. All I said was, 'This is over.' He didn't hurt me as much as Lucas did, so I considered it a win. He sent me notes afterwards saying that he was sorry, he had allowed himself to be carried away. That was why I didn't believe he would harm me when I went to Marco's. But like I said, I didn't know much about men.

I saw Marco by accident. Hohne had described him as 'my tame thug'. I watched his body language and it was clear both that Hohne had a complete hold over him but that he seethed with banked down anger and resentment. I recognised the emotions. And a tiger remains a tiger, even when in a cage. And I did notice the body under the suit and with my new-found knowledge, wondered what he might look like undressed. Pretty good, I reckoned. It was Hohne who told me what a looser Marco was, spending his afternoons sitting in cafés alone. 'Do you tail him?' I asked.

'Not now I know he is under my thumb.' Hohne looked disgustingly pleased with himself than added, 'He wouldn't dare challenge my authority.' All the more reason for me to make him my weapon, I thought. I did own a cat called Misty and she had recently died and I had loved her so when Marco 'accidently' came across me I was crying for real. I sat there and dredged up all of my emotions about when mum died and when I had to leave Misty's body at the vet's; isn't that what actors do? Put themselves into character and emote? I mean, acting is just lying by another name, isn't it. Something changed when he gathered me into his arms and rested his cheek on the top of my head. I had been fighting the world alone for so long and I did feel safe in that moment, and it was a lovely feeling, and those sobs were real, but I wasn't going to let emotion push me off course. Had I already considered that Marco might relieve me of my ex, well of course I had, though nothing went as I expected.

What I have never told anyone is that the knife Marco used to stab Lucas was mine. Not because I had noticed Lucas stalking me, because I hadn't, but I had been feeling uneasy. To be honest, it was the two men in the downstairs flat who I had assumed had put me on edge. Both were a bit pushy. Getting too close as I walked through the outer door, making it obvious that they were peering down the front of my blouse, 'accidently' brushing my backside as I passed them in the hallway, making half-audible comments when they passed; they did it all. Which is why they agreed to so much work when Lucas destroyed my apartment. They came up to peer through the police tape and be nosy.

When they saw all the blood and then I told them that when I was interviewed by the police I was going to mention that they had offered me an unwanted invitation for a sexual threesome, they were as good as gold. As if I would! The threesome, maybe, though not with them. Tell the police, never.

The knife was the largest I could find from a department store. I kept it at the end of my worksurface, laying in the open, ready to grab. When Lucas kicked my door down I was completely confused. I couldn't grasp where he had come from or why. And then he began shouting at me, all kinds of words and accusations. Nothing to the point, however. Only repeating about how he owned me and I belonged to him. Soon after we married he began doing 'social cocaine'. He would come home and tell me how wonderful it was. That was when my daydream of having someone in my life who loved and cared for me died completely. But I didn't ring Marco; I rang the police. It was only when they didn't come, I rang him. For a long while I didn't know why I did that. Rang in that order, that is.

When Marco decided to hike the Pacific Trail to hide until his brown skin returned to its natural colour I had no intention of being anywhere he could find me when he returned. I had the money. I no longer needed him. I had always thought that I had antisocial personality disorder, the proper term for a socio- or psychopath. But when Marco left, I grieved. The pain brought me to my knees. I had gone to him assuming him to be what Hohne called him, a dumb thug. The man who bedded me with such care and attention to my needs was loving, caring, and above all, lonely. And far more intelligent than he thought he was. He was a long way from Hohne's word 'dumb'. For the first time since my dad died when I was ten, I cared for someone. Oh, I loved my mum dearly, but the dementia had taken her mind away years ago, leaving me nothing but a shell who didn't know who I was. I finished grieving for her a long, long time before she died. I had few friends, and no one close. Lucas was a disappointment practically from when I moved in with him, the wedding lines still damp on the paper. Hohne had been sexually interesting, but I hadn't cared for him deeply.

The cruelty that underlay his nature was plain as day to me however well he treated me; and he did treat me well, on the whole.

Living without Marco was hell. I had manipulated and lied to him from the beginning. For weeks I hovered, wondering if he would ever forgive me if I confessed all? I was deeply and it felt irrevocably in love, but I was not who my lover believed me to be. That was seven years ago. When Marco arrived here, at first we were terrified. We lived like hermits, scared stiff and only venturing out for essentials. We were sure that an English woman with a huge dark-haired man would send out all sorts of signals to people; Interpol, Hohne's people who still floated around, other crooks, even those once belonging to Xaviera, but nothing happened, which in its own way was scary. And then I got on with ordering builders around and hunting for taps and light switches and furniture and all the other miscellaneous items housebuilding requires. By the time we had the house and garden settled, we had begun to relax, though I didn't touch Hohne's money for a lot longer. I had plenty of my own for the time being. Marco had his garden to build, but I became bored once the house was how I wanted it. So I began to search for the kind of people that knew about batteries, and green energy, and water recycling. And that is how my first business began, with the solar panels that could cope with this climate. The first five years flew by in a blink of an eye. And then there was the consolidation and major hurricanes and the clearing up afterwards. Time was fast flowing. Marco asked me to marry him a few times, but I brushed him off saying I was far too busy. The last time he asked was about ten months ago.

Since then, guilt has been festering inside me and growing as if it is yeasted. I have never told him any of this. I simply met him here in Barbados once he had muddied his trail to freedom and opened my arms to him. Now, here he comes at last, walking up the beach towards me in all his hunky beauty.

'Ah, my Evie, I am, I think, a little tired.' His grin is wide and wicked. And I hear my laugh and feel my joy. The breeze off the blue ocean blows the palms around, shushing their leaves as if they are confiding secrets. I just hope they don't know mine. We walk up through our garden brushing past brilliant flowers that bloom all year long, waving at Dusty who is sitting on her veranda grinning, as she knows exactly what we will be doing once we reach our own home. The air is both salty and perfumed. I hear myself giggle, like a silly girl, but that is how I feel. Loved and happy. If guilty.

We both shower outside in cold water. It is no penance. The water feels delicious running over our salty skin as the sun reaches long fingers into the water to try to dry us even as we stand under the deluge. Laughing, we walk into the house to find homemade lemonade and slouch for a while to let our bodies dry. Marco is watching me, his eyes lidded. He has pulled on some loose shorts and they tent at the front. I laugh out loud feeling as giddy a child. He stands over me and tugs me upright, and his kiss is so tender my guilt twists my guts. I kiss him back, hard and desperate, hoping he will think it is need, not fear.

We move to lay together in the bed and I pull off his shorts then kneel and take him in my mouth. His skin here is baby soft, and I stroke the tip of my tongue over the vein that pulses up the side. I take him deep and begin to suck in a way that pleases him. I know that I am trying to earn points so that he will not leave me. When his hands fist in my hair I release him and kiss my way up his body, tasting, nipping, making long wet trails that I then dry with my fingers. He watches me with a half-smile on his face until he loses patience and picks me up and flips me onto my back.

We make love on our expensive sheets, my skin luxuriating as it slides against them and satisfaction arcing inside me as he slides deep, then slowly pulls out. He holds his rhythm, feeling my own desire rise to meet him. As I begin to thrash he holds his pace for a while until I am frantic, and then he pounds into me, over and over again. I explode and only then does he seek his own release, which makes me pulse again, a vicious aftershock that wrings sensation out of the very air. I collapse, sated, stroking his sides lightly with my palms. Marco lies above me, his weight on his elbows, his legs imprisoning me. I breathe in a deep satisfied breath.

'What were you musing over down on the beach?' he asks. I smile up at him, his hair falling down, curtaining us in a private space inside our private home. Safe.

'Nothing,' I say.

'Were you thinking about our past?'

'What makes you say that?'

'Because when you think about our past, it is as if gravity is heavy on your shoulders.'

'What do you mean?' I swallow and my blood runs cold. I shift, but he has me imprisoned.

'Sweet Evie. I have been waiting for seven long years for you to tell me the truth. Oh, I haven't given it that much thought. When I arrived here I expected that you would have fled with all of the money. Initially I even doubted you would leave me a little to live on, but I wasn't concerned if you didn't. If you didn't want me I was resigned to letting you go.'

I stare up at him, now rigid with shock. What did he know, how much? I begin to wriggle, to try to flee.

'Lie still little one, you aren't going anywhere.' I search his face as memories of Lucas flood my mind, but Marco is still smiling down at me, his face gentle.

'Seven years?' I squeeze out through a dry throat and mouth.

'At first I thought about it a lot, but then I let fade away. You seemed happy, and there was no point in upsetting you, but I have begun to realise that lies fester. And I can feel them within you as if I can stroke them with my fingertips. I think perhaps they grow, and you don't need them. You believe yourself wicked, but you are not. I have let this go on too long.'

'What do you know?' I whisper.

'I didn't recognise you in the café. Oh, you looked a little familiar, but not much. It was when I held you I began to realise. You sobbed in my arms, and it was not the grief for a companion pet, however much loved. It was the pain I felt when I watched my brother die and my mama catch his body as he fell. Your grief and loneliness called to me, echoed within me. After the market I stalked you, hunted out your work place and your apartment. And then I broke in.'

'How?' Broke in? Marco is no housebreaker. This I can't believe.

He grins. 'A dad and his son sat with me in the café one day. They had bought a lock picking kit with instructions online, and it worked. The dad was so amazed at how easy it was, and a little worried I think, and they told me all about it. So, I copied them. And it was easy. And so one afternoon I roamed around your apartment and learned about you. And I saw the knife, sitting bold on the worksurface. Oh, and the heroin in your underwear drawer. I rubbed some on my gums. Believe me, many soldiers have been tempted by the illusion of escape from a war zone. Were you spiking Lucas' cocaine with it before you left?'

My throat is so dry all I can do is nod, but Marcos does not accept that. 'Why?' he asks.

I give a miserable shrug. 'If he was going to go to hell, I wanted him there quickly. I only added a tiny amount, I didn't want to murder him, just help him along a road he was already on.'

'I saw the toxicology report. He had no heroin in his system. He was hyped on cocaine and amphetamines when he attacked you. You had nothing to do with his drug use.'

'But Dusty. I stole her land. She never wanted to sell.'

'No, but she was alone and becoming frail, and too proud to ask for help. You invaded her life and helped her anyway. 'That fool girl,' she calls you. She has hardly spent a penny of the money you gave her for this site, she likes to open her account book and stroke the numbers with her fingers. She gets a real buzz about dying a millionaire. She would have given you the land for the way you had her home rebuilt exactly as it was, for all the care you gave her then and still give her. Why feel guilty? She hasn't cooked her main meal or had to buy groceries since you arrived. She thinks she is taking advantage of you, and loves to laugh about it. Hence the name 'fool girl'. But, and this is the most important 'but', she loves you. And,' he adds smugly, 'she loves me.' His wicked grin is right there, splashed across his face. More softly he adds, 'But she would like some little ones, as would I. What did Lucas really do to you?'

I begin to cry. Marco is right, the guilt has got worse since his last proposal. Marco swings lithely off me and gathers me into his arms. He holds me close and I feel his breath in my hair and I cling to him. Have I lost him? Was our lovemaking his farewell? My crying turns to sobbing.

'Hush, little one. Don't fret. It is you I want, and whatever life throws us, as long as we face it together. Tomorrow is Sunday, and my birthday, and the anniversary of seven years here in our new life. Seven is a mystical number, no?' My crying slows. Perhaps he does not despise me too much. 'I have let this go on for far too long. I hoped that ignoring it would make it disappear, but it hasn't, has it? Yes, I dropped Hohne off every Sunday, but because of that I began to make friends with the staff. I had glimpsed you and the staff described his woman. In time, I worked out that it was you who was Hohne's mistress. It was the high-heels that deceived me; you looked so accomplished in them. The Evie I met was a 'no-heels-and-proud' kind of woman. But when I saw the amazing underwear at your apartment, things began to click into place. Like the fact that you were willing to come to my apartment.'

'I didn't think Hohne would punish me if I was caught. He didn't care for me, but he had no illusions either. I was just a whore to him. If I switched my affections to his driver, he would most likely just despise me.'

'Maybe, but you took the risk. And that is the real point. I have seen how hard you have worked to make his evil money do good in the world. You have developed and supplied de-salination plants to peoples whose environments have been desiccated by climate change. Paid for forests to be planted, reefs to be regenerated. You never stop.'

'The money keeps on growing! The more I spend the more I make. I thought spending millions of pounds would be easy, but money really does grow more money!'

'Sweetheart, you can stop whenever you want. Stop now, and enjoy your life.'

'I'd be bored,' I mutter sulkily into his chest.

'I know. Now, do you love my Mama?'

'Of course.' How can he ask?

'What about my bull of a Tata?'

'I adore him!'

'I know, which is why tomorrow we marry.'

'Marry? I can't.' Marco is Catholic, and his faith is important to him, as it is to Mama and Tata. But me, I can't believe.

'You can and you will. I tattooed your name on my body, I want my ring on your finger. And it will make Mama and Tata happy.'

'But the priest?'

'We have had long talks. He would rather marry me to a sinner than watch me live permanently in sin. That is why I have waited. The foolish man believed I would grow tired of my godless woman and marry a fine Catholic girl. He had finally decided to give up and marry us as the best of all evils.'

'I will go to my own wedding, but I can't attend services every week, or ever. It would be every kind of wrong.' My tears have dried and I am beginning to hope. Can we do this? Will he? Can I? Confusion flies around my mind.

'My little Evie, you are not as wicked as you think. Lonely as well as alone; frightened; grieving, you were many things when I met you, but not wicked. I love you, have from the first and always will.'

'Marco!' I grasp his face in my hands, 'I finished with Hohne before I came to you. I swear.'

'I hoped, but had decided that it didn't matter, though, to be brutally honest, it did for a while. Men are territorial creatures, and I wanted you to be all mine. But I was a realist.'

His kiss is soft and gentle. 'Marry me, little Evie, but only if you love me.'

I am not about to marry the man of my dreams, as my dreams would have been too monochrome and unadventurous. I am about to shout to the world that this man is mine, and I am his. I kiss him back. Enthusiastically.

Marco wakes me the following morning with coffee and a wide grin. 'We are rich. How about we take a holiday and enjoy it?'

I blink. 'All of my money is tied up,' I say.

'But you haven't touched mine. Five hundred million kisses.'

I grin at the memory of the message I sent. I would happily give him a kiss for every pound or dollar.

He looks across to me, 'Is there anywhere you would like to go? Palm trees, sand and a soft ocean are all very well, but we deserve a break. We spent much of four of our years here putting the island back together after hurricanes.'

'What if we are spotted? Identified?' My guts feel cold.

'How will they? We have had surgery; we have left no real marker as 'rich people' on the Web or in the world. You had a seriously well-paid job in the past, as has Evalinda Hope. Your seed money for your businesses could have come from that.'

And suddenly if feels possible. And worth the risk. 'Florence. I want to see Italy. Drive down the Amalfi coast.'

'I want to show you my country. Beautiful Serbia. Not the dusty streets I grew up in, but the green hills and forests of my native land. Oh, and I want to taste caviar and really good champagne. Not every day, but just to try once.'

He licks his lips and grins, and I am grinning back. A flood of longing fills me. 'And a luxury hotel overlooking a Venetian canal. One with chandeliers and waiters who spread a white linen napkin on my lap before I eat.'

'A honeymoon in Italy then. I will arrange it. And now, we have to get up. Today we get married.

He pulls on my hand, but I stop him. 'Can I get a tattoo rather than wear a ring? One that says 'Marco'?'

'Only if I can buy you a massive diamond ring while we are away.'

'Done,' I say, and now I am grinning too. The past is gone. We have done, and will continue to do our best, but perhaps for a while we can have fun. And who knows, perhaps it is time to research if those little feet running around might be possible. I reach up and kiss my man. My beautiful, beloved, Marco.

Later we head for the church. I have a soft linen dress that floats around my calves and makes me smile, and carry a loose bunch of blue flowers. Marco wears blue cargo shorts and a white tee-shirt. I give a wide disbelieving grin. We look surprisingly stylish. He grins back, and we enter into the simple space of the church and gaze around. We know everyone. So many friends and well-wishers. Our wealth is here in the comfort they bring. As we stand to take our vows the priest is assisted by the only face I do not recognise. A dark-haired rather swarthy man is holding a large candle in a carved wooden holder. It is a rather romantic as well as religious gesture and I throw him a smile of thanks. Clearly, he is shy, as he drops his gaze. I turn back to Marco to make my promises, promises I know I will keep. Marco is in my soul. I have for him a depth of feeling I did not believe possible for me.

The service over we walk out into the sunshine and our future. And we are happy. Happy as few people ever are. Thank you Hohne, I whisper to the sky, and turn to kiss cheeks, and my wonderful husband.

Author's note

The story about the father and son who sent for a lock-picking kit and found it worked, is true. I was sitting at the next table in a café and I think the dad told me all about it because he was uncertain about what he felt about how easy it had all been.

Bibliography

If you want to know why all the 'bad' money in the world is headed to Nevada, read:

Moneyland, Why thieves and crooks now rule the world and how to take it back, Oliver Bullough, Profile Books, 2018, ISBN 978 1 78125 793 7

Acknowledgments

To Caroline, who read it through and simply said, 'brilliant'. Writing is a lonely profession, which is probably why most us who write like it, but some human support is wonderful. A pat on the back goes a long, long way towards making the hours of effort worth it. Also to Jaycee who deals with the tech. I am an absolute clutz when it comes to computers and coming across her was one of the best things that ever happened to me. Thank you to both of you. And to Becky and Janet, who both cheer me on. It means the world.

Book Group Questions

1. Does Evie deserve Marco?
2. Do you consider Evie a law-breaker when what she has stolen has been accrued by way of evil and criminality?
3. Evie wants to do what she considers good in the world. What would you do with multiple billions?
4. Why do you think she gave most of the money to the Goldintons?
5. How significant is it that when Lucas attacks her Evie rings the police, and only rings Marco when they are slow to arrive?
6. Has she got away with it?

Also by Meg Barber

Printed in Great Britain
by Amazon

35847788R00106